The Chronicles of Marr-nia

Short Stories Starring Barbara Marr

Karen Cantwell

COVER ART by Katerina Vamvasaki

Special thanks to my new friend and mentor, Maria E. Schneider. She's guided me generously through this last year.

Thanks also go to S. Wolf and JR Chase for sharing their brilliance and conjuring the amazing title for this collection.

ISBN 978-0-9837502-9-1

Author's Note

This collection of stories is short, but sweet. Contained here are four Barbara Marr shorts which I classify into two categories: Barbara Marr Life-of-a-Mother Short and Barbara Marr Mystery Short. If you've already read *Take the Monkeys and Run* and/or *Citizen Insane*, you will know that Barbara Marr is the protagonist of that series of humorous mysteries. If you haven't read *Take the Monkeys and Run* and/or *Citizen Insane* . . . well . . . hopefully you will want to after reading these stories!

I have also included two BONUS short stories that do not feature the character, Barbara Marr. The first BONUS story, "The Recollections of Rosabelle Raines," was first published in the mystery anthology, *Chesapeake Crimes: They Had it Comin'*. It is a personal favorite of mine, which is why I included it here. The second, "Sherman's Purpose," is my son's favorite, and so I present it here for you, and dedicate it to him.

To learn more about my other works, upcoming works being released, and to follow my blog, check out my website at www.karencantwell.com. I'd love to see you there!

If you enjoy this story, you may also like to hear the delightful audio version at www.Shortbreadstories.com

"Taming the Hulk" ～ •

A Barbara Marr Life-of-a-Mother Short

Mothers can relate to The Incredible Hulk.

We all have those gentle Bruce Banner moments where our lives and children are calm, enriching and fulfilling. Birds sing on our shoulder while we bake cookies and our well-mannered kids sip lemonade on the front porch. Life is good.

On the flip side are the moments that initiate the Hulk sequence. Kids fight over the remote control while the dog relieves himself on the new carpet. Simultaneously, the brutal rainstorm outside reveals more holes in the already-leaky roof and little Johnny's teacher is calling to ask why he hasn't turned in any homework for two months. Mothers lose control during those darker moments, and the thrashing green monster is unleashed. It's not a pretty sight, but it happens to the best of us. In fact, if any mother ever tells you she's never had a Hulk moment – she's lying.

My name is Barbara Marr and I am a mother who understands the Hulk phenomenon. I have been known to

Hulk-out. But one frustrating day, not too long ago, I stumbled upon an unlikely antidote: cheese balls.

At 5:25 p.m. on that fateful day, I had one headache, two doctor's visits to reschedule, three daughters giving me the evil eye, four piles of clean laundry screaming to be folded, and five minutes to get to ballet class which was twenty minutes across town. Husband Howard had called to tell me he would be working late for the eleventh night in a row. My pulse was increasing exponentially and the Hulk countdown had begun. My veins were turning green.

"I don't want to go to ballet today!" wailed my usually good-natured Amber, her blazing red curls accentuating her current temperament.

"Those lessons are expensive, young lady – you're going. I was dollars away from having to sell a kidney to pay for them." I pointed to the stairs. "Go get your bag."

I picked up the phone and punched in some numbers. "We'll go as soon as I reschedule these appointments."

Amber crossed her arms across her chest, stuck out her lip and glared me down before turning to stomp away.

A woman answered after three rings.

"Schmenck, Schmenck, and Yang Pediatrics, can I help you?"

"This is Barbara Marr. My daughters, Bethany and Callie, had appointments with Dr. Yang at four o'clock. You're not going to believe this – it sounds crazy, I know – but I couldn't find my car keys for over an hour. I turned the house upside down. That's why we missed those appointments. I have them now though – the keys, that is." I ended with a chuckle hoping to add some levity to an otherwise gruesome tale. "Can I resche . . ."

"I confirmed those appointments myself yesterday, Mrs. Marr. You should have mentioned then that you would be unable to keep them today."

This woman obviously didn't understand my situation. The Hulk doesn't like to be misunderstood. "No, I couldn't find my . . ."

"Our next available appointment is October 19th."

"But that's . . ." I counted on my fingers, " . . . five months away!"

"I can put you on our waiting list."

I sucked down a deep cleansing breath to hold the Hulk at bay. "But they need physical exams before they can go to summer camp. I have to turn the forms in next week."

"I can put you on our waiting list."

"You think I'm lying. I can tell you think I'm lying, but it's the truth. You should have seen me tearing the house apart looking for those keys. I finally found them in the freezer next to the peanut butter."

Bethany, my ten-year-old, plopped down in the chair in front of me, ballet bag over her shoulder, pen in one hand and notebook in the other. She leaned patiently against the kitchen table. Meanwhile, I kept fighting with the Nazi receptionist to secure appointments sometime sooner than the next solar eclipse.

My voice was starting to shake. "I was a freaked-out lunatic. Here, my daughter will tell you." I shoved the receiver in her face. "Tell her, Bethany."

"She was a freaked-out lunatic."

"It's true. I would never tell my daughter to lie for me. I need your help. I'm begging you."

"Would you like those appointments on October 19th?"

"No, you see, October is *after* summer. We need the exams *before* summer camp. Isn't there anything you can do for me?"

"I can put you on our waiting list."

Schmenck, Schmenck and Yang were celebrity pediatricians. Women got on a waiting list to be in their practice before conceiving. Northern Virginia Monthly ran an exclusive five-page article exalting their medical brilliance and business savvy. Supposedly they were the best in the area. Personally, I didn't see much difference from our other pediatrician. I mean, they gave the same shots and the same advice. It's not like they were handing out designer antibiotics. But I had pulled some tricky political strings to get in with these people, and I wasn't going to lose my prime status now by flipping out and upsetting the staunch gatekeeper.

"Yes, thank you. You're so kind." I hung up the phone and squeezed my head like a melon trying to relieve the constant throb.

"Mom, I need you to answer a survey question – it's for my homework."

Dropping my posterior in the chair next to hers, I peeked at my watch before laying my head on the table. We were now officially late for ballet lessons.

"They're still giving homework?" I asked. "School's almost over."

"Mrs. Pratt says she'll give homework right up till the last day. She says we have to constantly be learning because soon we'll have SATs to take, and that could make or break our choice of college which could affect our entire future."

"But you're only in the fourth grade."

"Mom, stay focused. What's your idea of the perfect day?"

"That's the survey question? Nothing about hypotenuses or the Big Bang Theory?"

"Mom . . ."

"Okay, give me a minute."

I rubbed my head again and closed my eyes. My perfect day. Today was not a perfect day. It was a nightmarish day. Thinking back though, so many days were like today. Running from lesson to lesson and tutor to doctor to orthodontist. There was always something and it was always important. Ballet was important for coordination and motor control – their pediatrician told me so. And piano lessons were critical for the learning process – their teacher told me so. Or maybe it was the child psychiatrist on the Today

5

Show. Who knew anymore? With so many "experts" out there, it was hard to keep track.

Then there was Amber. She was two points under the national average on her pre-reading skills test so the tutor was imperative – otherwise, she could be left behind eating the dust of millions of gifted kindergartners out there tearing through Harry Potter.

And I had my organic cooking class, "Cook Healthy, Raise Healthy Kids." Twice a week I barely made it to class on time to learn the value of feeding my children chemical-free foods rich in nutrients. I thought my new dishes were quite yummy, but the girls . . . they weren't so enamored. Once, I caught Amber sneaking over to her friend Penny's house for hot dogs and macaroni and cheese.

There were just so many things to know in this parenting game – so many things I had to do right, or it would all go wrong and they'd end up as homeless, cancer-ridden drug addicts begging for pennies on the corner of Despair Street and Loser Lane.

"Mommy! Callie called me an itchy shoe!"

I opened my eyes to find Amber two inches from my face.

"Shichimenchou you dope. Not itchy shoe." Callie joined Bethany and me for a sit-down at the kitchen table, her bent posture and grim face indicating her teenage displeasure with the world in general. A sophomore in high school, she loved confusing us all with foreign vocabulary words, courtesy her new favorite class, Japanese I.

"Translation please." I rubbed my temples. Hulk wanted out.

"Turkey. I called her a turkey. She stole my new purse and put bugs in it."

Amber's saucer eyes signified her innocence. "Not bugs – butterflies. At least they'll be butterflies one day. Probaally."

"Okay, quiet everybody. I need a minute to think. I'm helping Bethany with her homework. Then if we hightail it, we can still catch thirty minutes of ballet."

"I have homework too!" Amber crawled up in my lap and started poking my nose with her chubby little fingers.

"You are such a little freak show," Callie sneered.

"I'm supposed to count something in nature, so I chosed to count the freckles on Mommy's face. Now I need to start over. You broke my consummation."

"Concentration, dip brain."

"Mommy!"

My blood pressure was escalating second by second. I didn't want Hulk to show himself, but I didn't know if I could stop him. "Callie. Please, let her count."

As Amber slowly and meticulously touched and counted brown spots on my face, I watched hers. Her clear, perfect skin was just beginning to be speckled by the dots she inherited from me. Her bright, blue eyes shimmered as if they radiated light of their own. Her pink, pouty lips were

7

perfect by all accounts. I marveled at her sweet, warm breath on my face – still a child's breath, untouched by the ravages of time. I realized that it had been weeks, maybe even months, God forbid years, since I'd really looked at my sweet baby. A wave of calm blew through me and for a moment, Hulk receded.

" . . . fifty-three, fifty-four, fifty-five . . . Fifty-five! You have fifty-five freckles on your face." Amber leaned back, smiling proudly at her accomplishment. I pulled her in and kissed a soft cheek, then hugged her tight.

Callie sat across from me, her face propped up by her hand. No smile on her clear, lovely face, no sense of joy.

Bethany, a thing of beauty in her own right, was next to me glowering under a dark cloud of annoyance. She wanted an answer to her survey question.

What had I done to my children? To me? To our family? In my frantic need to do everything "right" and make their lives perfect, we had all ceased to be happy. We were scurrying around like rats in a maze, living by someone else's rules. And nothing was perfect.

I looked at my watch. If we jumped in the car that very minute and I ignored all posted speed limits, we could make it to ballet and still get thirty dollars' worth of lesson. I could still proudly tell the doctor that the girls get exercise every week and announce to neighboring mothers that my girls have never missed a ballet lesson at the Elite Academy of Dance. Ever. Hulk would have to appear to make that happen, and the girls would go to bed miserable, having seen Mom at her worst. Again.

Or . . . in what can only be described as a flash of brilliance, I got a better idea.

"Girls," I announced. "Change of plans."

"What does that mean?" asked Amber.

"We're scrapping ballet. Callie, be the sweetheart I know you can be and get the picnic blanket out of the upstairs closet."

She raised an eyebrow. "We're going on a picnic?"

"Of sorts."

Bethany did not look pleased. "I need to get this homework done."

"This is your homework. Trust me. You'll love it. And everyone bring pillows. Lots of pillows."

Amber was liking this game. "Can I wear my pajamas?"

"Wear whatever you want. Meet me at the front door in five minutes."

While the girls padded around the house collecting blankets and pillows and changing out of leotards, I grabbed a few items of my own and snuck them into a large brown paper bag. A Ziplock baggie finished off my list of necessary items.

At the front door, loaded down with pillows and blankets, the girls were waiting. I could tell by the looks on their faces that they were concerned their mother might be one step away from Loony Bin Central.

9

I opened the Ziplock baggie and held it out. "First, turn over all cell phones." Callie gave me her I'm-a-teenager-and-too-cool-for-this roll of the eyes, but slipped hers into the baggie anyway.

"Thank you. Now, anything electronic that plays music or video games, adds, subtracts, multiplies, downloads an 'app,' or pretends to be a dog, cat or alien pet from a distant dying planet."

The baggie filled to capacity as the girls pulled items from pockets I didn't know existed. I zipped it up and laid it aside.

"Now for the adventure. Everyone out and follow me." I didn't even wait for the questions and quizzical looks. I picked up my mysterious brown paper bag and marched to the backyard. The air was dry and warm. Prime for what I had planned.

I loved my backyard. The thick, green lawn stretched gracefully from the house until it met up with a line of trees that encircled the house. It was a major selling point when we bought the house – a large yard for the kids to run and play, private for special family times and also wonderful for entertaining. Yet we rarely even saw it anymore. Howard mowed it religiously every Saturday, treated it with fertilizer and weed killer, and then forgot about it until the next weekend. It was kind of sad, really. So well-cared-for, yet oddly neglected.

The girls arrived slowly, very confused, but they arrived.

"Can you lay out the blanket, Callie?"

"This is our adventure? The backyard?"

"Please – I really think you'll like this."

Reluctantly she laid out the used-once-only quilted picnic blanket. I moved to the center, put down the bag and sat my rumpus down.

"Come on, girls." I patted the blanket. "Sit."

Bethany and Amber sat first, hugging their pillows, joined by Callie, who sat on hers and hugged her knees. Ever so slowly, I pulled my surprise out of the paper bag. The girls stared, wide-eyed. They were speechless.

"What's that?" Amber asked, breaking the awed silence.

"I know what those are – those are cheese balls," answered Bethany. "Ashley Masters gets them in her lunch every day."

"Correct," I said opening the large cellophane bag. "These are cheese balls. They're made from over-processed corn-like products, artificial colors, artificial flavorings and MSG. None of which is good for you and all of which probably causes cancer in laboratory rats if you feed them enough. The beauty of the cheese ball is that it's smaller than its cousin, the cheese curl, and therefore, pops effortlessly into the mouth, just so." I munched on the crunchy prize, savoring its junk-food goodness.

"And you're going to let us eat them?" Bethany asked cautiously.

"Go for it."

All three girls smiled and grabbed for the bag. Within seconds, they looked like chipmunks, their cheeks bulging while they chewed. I pulled out a second bag and joined them in the munch-a-thon.

After a few minutes, I passed around cans of soda. "No junk food is complete without two thousand grams of sugar water to wash it down with." I gulped with pleasure. "Isn't this the life?"

"Where did you get this stuff?" Cheese powder spewed from Bethany's mouth as she spoke.

Sheepishly, I had to admit that I kept a stash of my favorite junk food hidden deep in my bedroom closet, partaking of the delicacies only after they were all asleep or at friends' houses. I thought the girls would be mad, but they just laughed.

"Is this supper?" Callie asked after a long swig on her drink.

"Sure. Why not?"

She looked at me oddly, then smiled. "Cool."

"And what do we do after this?" Bethany asked.

"That's the best part. Nothing. Absolutely nothing."

Amber beamed. "Boy, Bethany, I like your homework a whole lot. I can't wait until I'm a fourth grader."

Without caring about the clock, we lay on our blanket, heads on our pillows, watching the sun filter through green tree leaves, sparkling and dancing as it sank in the western sky. Yellows turned to golds, turned to blues turned to purples, and soon we were counting fire flies in the dark. We talked about our dreams, about fairies and leprechauns, whether trees can feel pain, what life would be like if we never grew up, and if it was really true that cats and dogs only see in black and white.

We held hands, rubbed backs and took turns braiding each other's hair. I learned that Bethany had a crush on Max Higgins, Callie thought her Japanese teacher was "kind of cute" and very smart, and Amber thought boys were "icky." The girls admitted that they all hated ballet, but Bethany thought singing lessons would be fun. We told stupid knock, knock jokes and laughed so hard that soda came out our noses.

If the phone rang, we never heard it.

If the Department of Homeland Security raised the terrorist threat level, we didn't know. We didn't care.

Life was good. Hulk was long gone.

And when Bethany turned in her homework assignment, she had only one answer to one survey question: "My mom's idea of the perfect day is eating cheese balls in our backyard until the sun goes down."

The very next day I called our old, less famous pediatrician who gladly gave us a timely appointment. Then I called Elite Academy of Dance and told them we wouldn't be returning for any more ballet classes. The fact that they wouldn't issue a refund didn't even register on my Richter scale. I had a long and calm talk with my husband, who agreed to less work and more family time. And that oddly neglected backyard – we spend hours out there now.

In retrospect, I realized something important. The antidote to a Hulk attack wasn't the cheese balls at all. It was what the cheese balls represented: love and fun. Simple ingredients, really.

After all, what is life if love isn't fun?

Just ask the Hulk.

"Top Lawn" ⁓ •

A Barbara Marr Life-of-a-Mother Short

The lawn was easily six inches high, we were expecting four straight days of rain, and my husband, Howard, had another twelve-hour day of work ahead of him. If someone didn't mow that grass soon, the town of Rustic Woods would be sending out a search and rescue team to find the missing Marr family, last seen in the jungle that was once their yard.

Howard was grabbing his keys while downing the last of his cold coffee.

"I think I saw a cheetah in our yard yesterday."

"What?"

"A cheetah. It was stalking a wildebeest. Can't be sure though, with the grass so tall."

"I'll try to get to it tonight."

"The cheetah?"

"You're so funny. The lawn."

"You said you'd be at the office late again."

"Yeah."

"Teach me."

15

"What?"

"Teach me to start the mower. I'll do it."

Howard slid me his typical I-don't-wanna-go-down-this-road look, but I pressed on. I was ready to tackle the bigger things in life. Truth be told, I'd never mowed a lawn in my life, and I felt rather unfulfilled. A bit unaccomplished.

I rubbed my hands together, anxious for some excitement. "I feel the need, the need for speed."

Howard wasn't amused. "Barb, it's a lawn mower. Is this really the time for a *Top Gun* quote?"

He'd crossed the line. I shook a finger in his face. "Any time is the right time for a *Top Gun* quote, Mister Man. Don't rain on my parade."

Howard rolled his eyes. "Now you're mixing your movie quotes. Go do what you do best – write a movie review and leave the lawn to a man."

Of course, that was the WRONG thing to say and he knew it. Five minutes later we were in our driveway with Howard giving me the one-minute course on starting a ten-year-old push lawn mower.

"Okay," I said, repeating the procedure out loud. "You push here a few times, pull there once or twice, flip this, snap that and push. Right? What's so hard about that?"

"You sure you don't want to wait for me to do it?"

"Howard. Four days of rain. By the time you get to this you'll need three machetes and a wilderness guide."

"Fine. You should wait a couple hours though. Let the sun dry it out a little more first."

Waiting was good. I sipped on a steamy cup of java, looked at the movie lineup on The Classic Movie Channel, fed the cat, threw in a load of laundry, and scraped up dried cereal goo off three different spots on my kitchen floor. Looking at my watch and draining my coffee cup, I decided the time was right. If I waited much longer, I would be late for my volunteer hour in Amber's kindergarten class. Couldn't do that – I'd be reprimanded. Not by the teacher. By Amber.

I slipped into my junkie sneaks and with the intention of Moses to part the Red Sea, stepped outside to confront and tame the great wild way. This was my day to show I was a real woman – that I was made of The Right Stuff.

The mower sat at the ready. I thought over the procedure once in my mind before committing the true act. Push a few times, pull once or twice, flip, snap and push. No problem.

So I pushed that button five or six times, thought better of it and pushed two more times just for good measure. Then I pulled. Didn't catch. That's okay. Howard said it could take a couple of times before I'd get the engine running. Pulled again. Hmm. That was twice. Again. Nothing. Maybe I wasn't pulling hard enough. I took a deep breath and yanked the cord with so much force, my shoulder nearly dislocated. Close, but it died before catching. I pulled four more times in succession, while screaming foul expletives only heard on HBO. Still, the trusty lawnmower was not cooperating with its new operator. I stood there, considering my options when I saw Mr. MacMillan headed my way. He had that poor-little-lady-doesn't-know-what-she's-doing look on his face.

"Barb! You need help with that thing?" he hollered from the end of my driveway.

That was all I needed. Pity from a man ignited the necessary spark within me. I would win this battle. With one long, swift, beautiful pull, that lawn mower engine caught like a catfish on a tasty worm.

"Nope, got it! Thanks, though!" I smiled and waved. So proud was I.

With a snap and a push, I was on my way. Moving the mower seemed a little harder than I had thought it would be. A lot harder, actually. I reasoned that it was due to the unusually tall grass. Yes, that had to be it. I pressed on.

After just two or three minutes, my hands felt like jelly and my arms screamed for mercy. This lawn mowing stuff was not the easy job I thought it would be. For years I watched Howard breeze through in no time, practically whistling while he worked. I mean, Howard does work out some, but he's certainly not the buffest stud around. How did he make this look so easy?

But I wasn't giving up. Women do this all of the time. Come on, Barb, I urged myself. Be a REAL woman.

Another five minutes later, sweat was blurring my vision and I felt like I'd just done ten hours bench pressing two-hundred-pound weights. And the tall grass was causing me more problems than just exhaustion. It kept stalling the mower. After four or five stalls, I finally figured out that I could prevent the stall by pushing down on the handle and lifting the mower up off the grass just as the engine started to choke. Problem was this often set me off course. Consequently, my lines weren't exactly . . . straight. No problem, I said to myself – I'll go back around and clean those up later.

Or not.

The exertion was just getting to be too much. I probably should have taken up body building before tackling lawn mowing. I ascertained that possibly changing my direction of mowing would alleviate the extreme pain I was experiencing. Instead of going up and down the lawn, I'd start going across. Couldn't hurt. Right?

What seemed like two days later, the lawn was only half-way mowed and I was ready for an ambulance ride to the ER. Not ready to give up, I opted for a brief break. I'd been sweating so profusely, I was in desperate need of some water and possibly a saline infusion.

The air conditioning inside was so nice. And the gallon of ice-cold water helped as well. Maybe, I thought, I should leave the rest to Howard. Of course, that would be admitting defeat. I looked at my watch. If I went back out right away, I could finish the job then pop in for a quick shower, dry off and dress, jump into the car and still be at Amber's class in time for my volunteer hour.

Deep breaths. You can do this Barb. Get out there. Tackle that Green Mile.

I threw my last glass of water on my face and trudged outside determined to slay this dragon. Back in front of the mower, I went through the routine again. I pushed here a few times, pulled there once or twice, the engine caught, and . . . hmmm. What was that? Flip. There was something to flip. Howard had mentioned it before, but I suddenly remembered missing that step on my own run. I looked closer at the lever I had forgotten to flip. It read, "Automatic Drive." Oops. Bet that automatic function would have made my first attempt a tad easier. I flipped. Then I snapped. And that darned lawn mower practically took off on its own. I probably could have pushed the thing with my thoughts, and certainly using my hands and arms felt like a breeze.

Yee-haw! I'd found the magic to lawn moving. "Automatic Drive." Wouldn't miss that step again. Now my only decision was, which way to mow? I'd done part of the lawn in one direction, and the other part perpendicular to that. Well, sort of perpendicular. I opted for a different angle altogether, reasoning that I could do the whole darned thing in that one direction now that it was so easy and Howard would never know I'd had a problem. Off I went, singing a little song and dancing a little dance. Baby animals sat and watched me with smiles on their baby animal faces and happy birds flew around me. It was a scene right out of a Disney movie. But somewhere along the way, I lost track of my lines. They were all mixed up now – going every which way. I was stumped. Then I looked at my watch.

Damn! Amber's class. I couldn't be late. I shut off the mower and pushed it into the garage.

I took one more look at my work before heading out to the school. It didn't look SO bad. Not really. Probably no one would even notice.

Since my volunteer hour was at the end of the school day, I drove both Amber and Bethany home with me. As we pulled into the driveway, Bethany spoke up.

"Uh, Mom," she said slowly. "WHO mowed the lawn?"

"Me," the pride obvious in my voice. "What do you think?"

"It looks all chopped up," Amber declared. "Did you use the lawn mower or a weed whacker?"

My daughter. The kindergarten comedienne.

"Does it look that bad?" I asked.

"It looks like a gorilla did it," Bethany decided. "A sick gorilla."

"Thanks."

"A sick gorilla with only one arm!" laughed Amber. The two of them were on a roll in the back seat, laughing away at their own jokes.

"Fine! I get it."

The three of us piled out of the car, the girls still giggling, and we stared at the monstrosity. Yikes. It looked worse than bad. What was I going to do? Howard would take one look at this and the next thing I knew, he'd be doing his Ricky Ricardo imitation.

I took off to the gardening shed. "Come on girls," I said. "We gotta fix this fast."

"We?" they groaned.

"I'll buy you ice cream after."

They'd do just about anything for ice cream. I had me two helpers.

"We only have a couple of hours before Daddy gets home, so start clipping." I handed them each a pair of small hand clippers. "Don't point them at each other."

Down on my knees, I started with my own set, clipping away at the grass. The girls followed suit, but seemed confused.

"What exactly are we supposed to be doing?" asked Bethany.

"Evening it up. Clip . . . clip where it looks uneven."

She didn't look convinced, but started clipping anyway.

So there we were, a half-hour later, crawling around on our grass snipping at errant blades of grass. My hands were cramping and my knees ached.

"I want my ice cream now!" whined Amber, as she fell back on her poor little bottom.

I was ready to give up and accept my fate. I'd failed, and Howard would freak. That's when Callie walked up with an angel. His name was Brandon.

"Mom. What are you doing?" Callie had that annoyed tone in her voice that only a teenager can have. Her friend, Brandon stood next to her. He looked amused.

"Fixing the lawn."

"Mommy mowed it," said Amber, "but as you can see, there were problems."

"You want me to fix that for you, Mrs. Marr?" Brandon offered.

"You can fix this?"

"Sure. Mow lawns every weekend in my neighborhood. I usually charge thirty dollars, but for you, I'll do it for free. You look like you need it."

I did need it.

Even though he protested, I paid that wonderful Brandon forty-five dollars and bought everyone a round of ice cream.

When Howard came home, he smiled and said, "Wow. Great job. Better than me. I think you should mow the lawn from now on."

Uh oh. Didn't see that coming.

Now I know what you're thinking. You're thinking I paid Brandon thirty dollars every week to come by and mow my lawn on the sly. Well, I'm sneaky, but I have my pride too. So, no. That's not exactly what I did.

I paid him, alright. Paid him to be my instructor. My Top Lawn instructor. We had our own Top Lawn School. He showed me the quickest and easiest way to start the mower, how to navigate a smooth and clean landing onto the lawn, steering the machine just right to cut in perfect, seamless lines. In no time, I was at the top of my class. Okay, I was the only one in my class, but I was getting all A's, baby. All A's. And one grand day, I graduated. I was on my own. Me. Marr-verick.

On graduation day, he gave me my official Top Lawn baseball cap.

"Gee, Viper, you shouldn't have."

Brandon acted his usual uncomfortable teen-boy self. "Um . . . I didn't really. You made it, remember?"

"Let me have my fun."

He shuffled his feet back and forth. "Mrs. Marr?"

"Yup."

"Do you have to keep calling me that? Now that we're done, I mean?"

"Viper?"

"Right."

"It's your call name. We all have call names in Top Lawn School. You're Viper and I'm Marr-verick. You don't like it?"

"Not really."

"Shoot."

He was such a nice, polite boy. Nearly a man, really. He shuffled a little again, looking at his feet uncomfortably, then up at me. "Well, if it's really important to you . . ."

I gave him a friendly punch. "I'm just teasing. Thanks for teaching me the ropes. Callie's in the house if you want to see her."

He turned to walk away.

"Hey, Brandon."

Turning back, he looked worried.

"You can be my wingman any day."

He smiled.

I stood, admiring my work. Fresh-cut, clean lines. Only a golf course could look better. I had become a pro. It was my turn to smile. And as I did so, Howard's Camry pulled into the driveway. As he climbed out and walked my way, I wondered if I should tell him the truth about my whole lawn mowing experience.

As he stood next to me, he took a look at the lawn, then at my hat.

"Top Lawn? What's that about?"

I hesitated. Should I?

Naw.

"It's classified. I could tell you, but then I'd have to kill you."

He rolled his eyes. "Have your fun." He stepped out onto the grass and surveyed my work. "Nice, I must say. And it's a relief having one less thing to do around here."

Now I HAD seen that coming.

I shook my head and turned toward the house. "Follow me, Mr. Man," I said, an evil grin on my face. "I'm going to teach you how to use a washing machine."

"The Road to Shangri-La" ⌣·

A Barbara Marr Life-of-a-Mother Short

Shangri-La. A harmonious valley; an earthly paradise; eternal happiness. Every mother has her Shangri-La.

Mine is like that commercial – you know the one. The kids are flying kites in the park on a crisp, sunny day while the parents lie back on a blanket with identical isn't-life-perfect smiles on their faces. Then the kids drop their kites and come running to their Barbie and Ken parents, jumping on them while everyone laughs. Love is abundant and emotionally stirring music plays in the background. I never quite understood how all of that relates to the athlete's foot cream they are advertising, but I don't care. I want to be just like them. Happy.

My name is Barbara Marr, and I'm a hopelessly optimistic mother in search of her Shangri-La.

***

"Howard, let's do it," I said that Friday night.

27

He smiled. "Sure. You get the girls to bed, I'll pour two glasses of wine and meet you upstairs."

"No, the Cherry Blossom Festival."

The smile disappeared and Howard rolled his eyes. "Bararb," he whined. "Why do you always do this to yourself?"

"Come on! It'll be fun. We've never gone."

"There's a reason for that. It's called 'Ten million people descend upon Washington, DC.' You know I hate crowds."

"No, look," I showed him the paper, "they tell you how to avoid the crowds."

"There's no way to avoid the crowds at cherry blossom time."

I shook my head and showed him the newspaper article I was reading. "The trick is in when you arrive at the Metro station."

"The Metro?!" He stood up. "No. No Metro trains. No Cherry Blossom Festival. I'm putting my foot down."

The room went silent.

The kitchen clock ticked and then it tocked. Tick, tock. Tick, tock.

"Howard." I took a beat. "How long have we been married?"

"Fifty years?"

"Seventeen."

"Right."

"In those seventeen years, what happens every time you put your foot down?"

He sighed. "You win?"

"Good. Now that we have that settled, we'll need to pack some supplies. We should be at the Metro station by seven a.m."

"Any chance we could still put the girls to bed and enjoy some . . . wine?"

"Let's see how tired I am after I get the supplies together."

At midnight, Howard was asleep and I was still following the instructions in the "Weekend" article on how to pack so you'd save time and money. Backpacks with water bottles, energy bars and Ziplock bags filled with popcorn. Antibacterial wipes, sunscreen and baseball hats to keep the sun off our faces. For lunch, to avoid the high cost and low quality of the fast food, I made sandwiches: turkey for Howard and me, BLT minus the B for Callie, since she was going through a vegetarian phase – added some cheese for protein. Hummus, cucumber, spiced beef and tzatziki sauce for Bethany – another phase. And PB&J for Amber, crusts cut off. One Ziplock baggie full of grapes another full of carrots, and voila! We were healthy and fed for lunch. Of course, what lunch is complete without a little dessert, right? The article was emphatic on this: to avoid the lines at the popsicle and ice cream vendors, pack your own special treat: frozen bananas. Luckily, I had a batch of ripe ones sitting on my counter. No popsicle sticks though, so I used wooden kabob skewers instead. I'm so smart. And I couldn't forget the kites. I stuffed everything except the frozen items into five backpacks and crawled into bed at one a.m., tired, but excited for the family adventure that awaited us. My Shangri-La.

Howard groaned when I cuddled up next to him.

"You done?"

"Yup. We're ready to go."

"Do the girls know?"

"Nope. I decided to surprise them in the morning."

He rolled over and mumbled something about surprises not being any fun, then quickly fell into a heavy snore.

***

"What?!" Callie screamed. "You made plans without asking me? I'm going to the movies with Emily and Brandon today."

Bethany rubbed her eyes. "I can't go. I have homework."

"Dora the Explorer has pickles in her backpack for Junie B. Jones but I don't know where the wild things are," whispered Amber.

I addressed them all with certainty: "Callie, you can go to the movies another time; Bethany, you can do it when we get home; and," I snapped my fingers in front of Amber's face, "wake up sweetie, you're still asleep." Amber has an odd habit of opening her eyes, but not waking up. "Now, everyone, get dressed and downstairs for breakfast so we can leave by six thirty."

Moans and groans shook the house worse than my twenty-five-year-old washer when the load is unbalanced.

"Don't go acting all spoiled. You should feel privileged. Poor children in the slums of Mumbai would kill to have the opportunity to see such beauty."

More moans and groans.

"Mom," whined Bethany. "Would you stop with the slums of Mumbai thing? We get it already."

True, I had gone a little overboard after seeing *Slum Dog Millionaire*. But all three stomped off to get dressed, so it must have worked.

Or not.

Six thirty had me ready at the front door, keys in hand, stomping my foot. I was alone.

Grrrrr.

Six thirty-one.

Crickets.

Six thirty-two.

"Hello?" I called up the stairs.

A thump gave me some hope that humans would appear soon.

Unfortunately, it was a lone thump.

Six thirty-three and my blood pressure was rising. We were pushing the envelope of the whole get-to-the-Metro-early part of the equation for a happy, crowd-free day in DC.

I needed some leverage to get this show on the road. Moms know about leverage. I yelled upstairs again, this time banging on the wall for added emphasis.

"If I don't see bodies down here right now, I'm taking away the Disney Channel, Harry Potter and Facebook. For TWO weeks!"

Thump! Thump! Wump! Bang! Bonk! Splat!

Three girls stood before me frowny and out of breath, but dressed for the weather. I'd take it. But no Howard. I called upstairs one more time.

"Don't make me say what I'll take away from you, oh Man of the House!"

Callie rolled her eyes, and Howard sailed down the stairs faster than Flash Gordon on uppers.

It works every time.

***

The ride to the Metro station was uneventful except for my not-so-subtle sighs every time we hit a stop light along the way. Each stop light cost us precious time. And then there was the road work and detour we didn't expect. What should have been a seven o'clock arrival time to the Metro parking lot was turning into a seven-thirty arrival time. Minutes can be like hours or even days when you're trying to avoid crowds. I looked at my watch. Seven twenty-eight. I sighed again and tapped my fingers on my armrest.

"What?" Howard asked, acting like he didn't know what was bothering me.

"You know what."

"It'll be fine."

"It won't be fine. The lines will be three times as long now. We'll have trouble finding parking."

"No we won't."

A block from the station, he turned onto the road for the Metro parking lot. We came to an immediate stop – because of the long line of cars waiting to get into . . . the Metro parking lot.

My sigh was so big and so long, I nearly passed out.

"What? We'll get in." He was way too confident for his own good.

I crossed my arms. "No we won't."

Ten minutes later, there was just one car between us and the automatic ticket kiosk. Howard was smirking next to me.

"Told you we'd get in." The gate lifted, allowing the car ahead of us through, then fell back down. Howard moved up and pushed the red button on the kiosk. It beeped at him. He pushed again. It beeped again. The gate wasn't moving.

"Shit!" he muttered under his breath. But I heard him.

"Full?" I asked.

No answer.

"I won't say it," I whispered, forcing back another sigh.

"What isn't Mommy going to say?" Amber yelled from her seat behind me.

"I told you so," answered Bethany.

"Oh," Amber nodded knowingly for all of her five years on this earth. "Guess that's 'cuz she says it so much, she's tired, huh?"

Howard's face glowed redder than a hot chili pepper. "Might I point out," he said through gritted teeth, "that I'm the one who said this wasn't a good idea to begin with? Who's right there? Huh?"

Cars behind us started honking.

"Now is not the time, Howard . . ."

"Oh, because when you're right, it IS the time, but when I'm right it's not the time?" A throbbing purple vein popped out on his forehead.

"I was ready at six thirty this morning, remember? If we'd gotten on the road at the designated hour . . ."

HONK! A veritable caravan of cars was now letting us know they were unhappy.

Howard exploded. "Aaahh!!" He jumped out of the van and flung his arms in the air like a wild man. He was screaming at the top of his lungs. "It's full! The parking lot is full!"

The honking stopped, but I feared the police might have been called as well. I dared not say another word.

It took us eight more minutes to convince enough cars to back up so we could maneuver out and seek parking along the road. At eight eleven a.m., we finally agreed (after some loud "debate") that the high school parking lot several blocks away was the only available alternative. Those spots were going fast too, so we grabbed up a spot in what looked like possibly the last row in the farthest back corner of the school lots, parked and piled out the van. There wasn't one smile on one face in our little family of five as we trudged off, burdened by heavy backpacks. Shangri-La seemed distant at best.

Howard predicted the walk to the station to be five minutes or less which should have put us there by eight sixteen.

At eight forty-one, we found ourselves in another line. This time for train tickets.

At nine a.m., after five people in front of us had to ask assistance in operating the ticket machines, we were finally standing on the platform waiting for the next train into Washington, DC. I had to hold onto both Bethany and Amber for fear of losing them in the dense crowd of other people also seeking a day of fun and beauty. Soon, I thought, soon, we'd be standing under the cherry blossom trees, light pink petals raining down on us while we all giggled with joy. This day would get better yet. I just knew it would.

"I can't breathe!" hollered Bethany, whose face was nearly plastered to the rather round and very large bottom in front of her.

It was true. With each minute, the crowd got tighter and tighter until I felt like that last pair of socks being shoved into the already-packed-too-full suitcase.

I felt a tugging on my sleeve. It was Amber. She was saying something, but I couldn't hear her.

"What?" I shouted.

She yelled (I think), but the sound was drowned by the roar of the crowd. I bent down, getting my ear as close to her mouth as I could. "What?"

"I have to go pee pee."

Crap.

"Can you hold it?"

"How long?" she asked with a frightened look on her face.

I looked again at the crowd. The train still hadn't arrived and as far back as we were, we weren't going to make it onto the next one and we'd be lucky if we'd make it onto the one after that.

"An hour? Maybe an hour and a half?"

She danced a little, winced, and then her little face puckered up ready for a cry. My Mommy's Heart did a flip-flop and as every mother knows, that's where the rubber meets the road. I grabbed her up.

"Come on everyone! We've got to find a bathroom."

The masses of people had seemed to jell into a sort of single-cell-like unit, and it wasn't releasing the Marr family easily. I stepped on at least six toes and said "Excuse me" no fewer than ten times. Back up the escalators we went. After several minutes of unsuccessfully spotting a door that said "Ladies" or a sign that said "Restrooms," I found a booth behind a glass window with a sign above that read, "Information."

"Where are the restrooms?" I asked the stone-faced man behind the glass.

"Ain't any."

"Hmm?" Surely I had misheard him.

"Ain't any."

I raised my voice a little higher and enunciated more clearly, convinced he didn't understand my question.

"REST . . ROOMS. Where ARE THEY?"

"Ain't any. Didn't you hear me the first time?"

My jaw dropped.

"You don't have any restrooms!?"

Amber's legs were crossed and she started dancing again.

Howard and Callie, who had gone off themselves looking for some facilities, returned and stood behind me.

"What's going on?" Howard asked.

I turned and screamed in his face. "Ain't any!"

He wiped a drop of spit from his nose. "Why are you yelling at me?"

I spun around, then quickly changed tactics and put a sweet smile on my desperate mother face. "My five-year-old has to go to the bathroom – she *has* to go. I'm sure you understand the urgency. Five-year-olds can't wait. Could she use your bathroom?"

"Ain't no public restrooms in the station."

A deep, cleansing breath was in order. And possibly a shot of tequila.

"Right. I understand. But *you* have to go during the day. Could she use *your* bathroom? Please?"

"I'm only going to say this one more time, then you are going to have to step aside so I can help someone else. There AIN'T NO PUBLIC RESTROOMS IN THE STATION. You will need to go somewhere else."

Somewhere else?

This man was lucky he was standing behind a glass partition. I had hands and felt ready to wrap them furiously around his thick neck.

"Where then, sir would we find a public restroom nearby?"

"I don't have that kind of information Ma'am. Step aside please."

An explosion went off within me. I'd been sent over the edge. Like Shirley MacLaine in *Terms of Endearment* when she wants her daughter to get her pain medication, the rant was simply beyond my control.

"I should just let her pee her pants right here all over your floor, is that what you'd like? Huh? Then you'd have to deal with it, wouldn't you? Is that what people do around here when they can't find a bathroom – just pee on your floor!?"

Howard rolled his eyes and started pulling me away.

"Barb . . ."

Callie was covering her face.

"Mom . . ."

"Sorry," Howard said to Stone-face.

"Sorry!?" I shouted loud enough for the Space Shuttle to hear. "Sorry?! Don't tell him you're sorry! That man has a bathroom and he's not sharing!"

Callie took off ahead to distance herself from her raving lunatic of a mother, and Bethany wasn't far behind. Howard was pulling me away toward the exit with poor little Amber in tow, bravely bearing the embarrassment I had just caused her.

So the Metro station wasn't Shangri-La. It was the anti-Shangri-La.

Outside, with fresh air to help calm my frazzled nerves, I set myself to solving our new problem. I scanned up one side of the street and down the other. Nothing but cars in parking lots as far as the eye could see on our side, and an endless line of townhouses on the other. No gas station. No flashing red sign that said, "Restrooms HERE!"

"Let's go." I grabbed Amber's hand and started walking.

Everyone else followed.

"Where?" Bethany whined.

"Back to the car. If we find a bathroom on the way, great. Heck, I might stop at one of those townhouses and knock on the door if it gets really bad." I looked at Amber. "You okay, sweetie? Can you hold it?"

Her eyes were rimmed in red, and she was biting her lip. All she could do was nod. My poor baby. When this was all over, I'd make them pay. I'd go to every news station and newspaper in the DC metropolitan area, exposing them for their intolerant practices. Headlines would read: "Metro Turns Its Back on the Incontinent. Mother Fights for Justice." The story would go national and soon I'd be sitting on a couch talking to Matt Lauer, who would feel my pain. Metro would be screaming for mercy, apologizing publicly while simultaneously installing state-of-the-art public restrooms in all of its stations. A Metro spokesperson would thank me, Barbara Marr, on the Oprah show for bringing this horrid lack of sensitivity on Metro's part to the public eye.

We had all been walking as fast as little Amber's feet could go and I was lost in my Metro Revenge reverie when Bethany pointed and hollered out at the top of her lungs. "Look! Look at the playground!"

Nearly at the end of my rope, I lashed out. "Bethany. Does it look like we have the luxury of time to be wasting at a playground so you can have a little fun?"

Bethany's face blanched at my fury and she shrunk back.

"Mom," whispered Callie. "I think she means to point out the building NEXT to the playground."

Howard nodded. "Looks like bathrooms to me."

It was my turn to shrink. Slowly, I turned my head, and there, to my wondrous eyes did appear a little playground at the base of a grassy hill, and next to that playground was a building made of brick that had the familiar appearance of a public restroom. I sent Amber running toward it.

"Go, Sweetie – we'll catch up."

Callie explored while Bethany sat morosely on a swing. I looked at my watch for the first time since we'd left the station. The groan was automatic. "Nine forty-five," I said to Howard.

"It will be ten thirty before we get on a train. If we're lucky."

"After eleven before we get off that train."

"Another twenty minutes to walk to the tidal basin to see the blossoms."

"We'll be tired and hungry and cranky."

"And we won't miss the crowds."

I felt defeated. As if the God of Family Fun had spit on us. My dream of Shangri-La, dashed.

Amber skipped from the little brick building with a smile on her face. She was ready to go again.

"Hey!" Callie was calling from the top of the little hill behind the building. "Come here!" There was a playfulness in her tone that I hadn't heard since she'd hit puberty. I gave Howard a shrug and the two of us headed her way, with Amber and Bethany passing by, leaving us in the dust. By the time we reached the three girls, I was huffing and he was puffing.

"Look! We don't have to take the Metro after all," Callie said with the happiest grin I'd seen on her face in years.

Amber and Bethany were jumping up and down, shrieking in glee.

It was a miracle.

I smiled.

Howard smiled.

I felt like Peter Finch in the movie *Lost Horizon*, standing at the rim of the mountain looking down into paradise. We'd found our cherry blossoms. I had my Shangri-La.

And it appeared to be our own little secret, save for a few others who dotted the landscape.

As it turned out the playground and adjoining public restroom were only a very small part of the larger, grassy park that lay on the other side of the hill. And what encircled that grassy park? Pink and white blossoms. In what must have been a mimic of the Washington, DC Tidal Basin landscaping, easily a hundred cherry trees grew around the circumference of the park.

The girls tore happily down the hill.

Howard and I exchanged glances.

"I think I'm going to like it here," I said.

"No crowds on the Metro?"

I sighed in relief. "No crowds on the Metro."

The air was warming nicely as we made our way down to the center of the grassy dell, and a gentle breeze kissed my face. Howard and I pulled a thin blanket from one of the backpacks and sat while the girls danced under blossoms that floated to the ground like pink rain.

We stayed all day, eating our yummy sandwiches and frozen bananas, soaking in the sun and throwing a Frisbee. The little hidden gem of a park even attracted a funny juggler and a couple of musicians. And there was kite flying, just like the happy foot cream commercial. For that moment in time, our life was perfect.

"I told you it would be fun," I said to Howard as we packed up to leave.

He squinted at me. "You only remember the good things."

I nodded. "The good things. Shangri-La."

"Missing Impossible"

A Barbara Marr Mystery Short

We were on a stakeout. The very air around us was electric with the excitement of potential danger. On the edge of my seat with anticipation, my mind was ablaze with rich and vivid imaginings of what wild adventure might lay ahead.

Right. In the movies maybe.

Here, not so much.

We were on a stakeout alright, but it wasn't exciting. It wasn't even mildly interesting. I had hoped for more. I had hoped for sparking electric air. I had dreamed of anticipation and the need to calculate some necessary mission-oriented action at a moment's notice. Instead, what I got was a cold cup of coffee in a stinky Buick while I sat shivering as the thermostat on the bank across the street read thirty-eight degrees. That was in the sun. We were in the shade. Damn!

"What's that awful smell?"

"Dunno," answered Colt. "Something in the trash, I guess."

"Trash?"

"In the trunk," he said matter-of-factly, as if I would understand.

I didn't understand. This required further inquiry.

"Why is there trash in the trunk of your car?" I asked, trying to disguise my disgust.

"Part of the routine, Curly," Colt mumbled while simultaneously chewing a Boston cream donut. "Always check their trash. Once they put it on the street, it's public property. I grabbed hers on the way over to pick you up – put it in the trunk. We'll go through it later." He sipped from his cup and swallowed down the last of his donut. I wondered if his coffee had turned to slushy ice like mine had.

Colt Baron. He's a private investigator. To know him is to love him. All women do. My daughters love him, my friends love him, my mother loves him – although that wasn't always the case – and of course, I love him. Problem is, I have a husband. If that weren't complicated enough, Colt and my husband, Howard, were currently roommates in a two-bedroom condo across town. Long story. I could write a book on that one.

My name is Barbara Marr. Most people just call me Barb, except for Colt, who calls me Curly. To state the obvious – because I have curly hair. The hair was once a sad mousy brown, but now belies my age as more and more dismal gray strands creep their evil way into the fray. On a good hair day with some wash-in color, I can look a tad like Sarah Jessica Parker. On a bad hair day I look like Don King's long lost white sister. But I'm forty-five years old and have birthed three children. Who cares about a little messy hair? Let's face it – after a woman has presented herself panting and prostrate on a table with her legs in stirrups, with half the hospital staff viewing her wares every five minutes, a bad hair day is a walk in the park.

Back to the stinky Buick.

So there we were, Colt looking as handsome as ever with his yellow, wispy, want-to-run-your-fingers-through-it hair (nary a gray strand in sight), and me – old, cold, and grumpy – contemplating the idea of rifling through putrid bags of trash. So much for excitement. Unless we found an unclaimed winning twenty-million dollar lotto ticket stuck to that messy (ahem) feminine product, the prospect seemed way less than attractive.

"We're going to go digging through someone's trash?" I moaned, unable to hide the disgust any longer. "This isn't exactly what I thought investigating would be like. Why did you drag me into this?"

"Drag you?" Colt glared me down. "You begged me, remember?"

"Well, 'beg' is a strong word." Pouting now, I slumped further down in my seat, working my coat around me as closely as I could to stave off the inevitable hypothermia.

"Wanna donut?" Colt said, shoving a Donut King bag in front of my frowny face. I was too cold to eat – the act itself would require me to expose my hands to the frigid air and possible frost bite. I shook my head and shoved the bag away with my elbow.

"Boy, you're Miss Personality today," he said. "You want me to take you home?"

"No. I asked to be a part of this. I'll stick it through. Just thought it would be a little more . . . interesting."

"I told you it wasn't exciting or glamorous work, remember? No Magnum. No guns. No red Ferrari. No car chases. This is it, Curly. Sitting, sometimes for hours on end, waiting for some woman's lover to show up – or not – snap a few pictures if we're lucky, cash a check. If the check doesn't bounce, we celebrate with a Corona until the next client comes along."

"Yeah, but you didn't say anything about trash."

"True. Sorry 'bout that."

I looked at my watch and then out through the windshield at the two story garden apartment building we'd been surveilling. An hour and twenty minutes. She'd gone into that apartment an hour and twenty minutes ago. No one else had followed. I sighed and watched as my breath turned visible. In the arctic-like air, an hour and twenty minutes felt like a year and twenty days.

"What's this chick's name again?" I asked.

"Paula. Paula Duffy."

"Her picture looks so familiar, but that name just doesn't ring a bell. Why does her husband think she's cheating?"

"This apartment we're watching. She's been renting it for over year. He only found out about it – accidentally – three weeks ago. She doesn't know he knows."

Now THAT was juicy info. Who can turn down a story like a woman gone bad?

"Cool," I said. "You think her stud is in there right now or you think he'll be along soon?"

"Bingo! Take a look for yourself, Curly – here comes stud-boy now." Colt was pointing at the apartment while positioning his telephoto lens at the ready. Unraveling myself from my coat cocoon, I grabbed the binoculars from the floor to get a better look.

A taut, squat Asian man was knocking on the door. The frame was familiar, but I didn't have a full view of his face. If only he'd turn around a little bit more . . .

"Colt! I know that man!"

"What?"

"Give me that picture! Let me see her face again."

Still snapping the shutter furiously, Colt threw the glossy colored photo my way. I looked at it, and immediately remembered who she was.

"It's Parra!"

"Who? What?"

"Parra. From Tae Kwon Do. That man knocking on her door is Master Kyo. He owns the place. And she's Parra – his shining star student. Parra is having an affair with Master Kyo! How fun is that?" I was beginning to warm up nicely. This investigation stuff was invigorating after all.

The door opened and Master Kyo stepped in. Unfortunately, it was impossible, even with the binoculars, to see who had opened the door.

"Curly, her name is Paula – not Parra."

It took me a minute to understand what he meant, but then it all became crystal clear, and boy, did I feel stupid. Certainly, it sounded like Parra when Master Kyo spoke, but then again, when he yelled at me, it sounded like he was telling Bob, not Barb, to do twenty push-ups. I thought back over the many times I had called her Parra to her face. "Hi, Parra, how are you?" "Hey, Parra, great kick!" "Ow! Parra, that hurts – don't kick so hard!" My face went red when reflecting upon my many Parra faux pas. And yet, she had never corrected me.

The door had closed, leaving us with nothing but the view of a dingy apartment once again. A few silent minutes ticked by.

"Did you get any good, incriminating pictures?" I asked finally.

"Dunno. We'll stick it out here and wait for one or the both of them to leave . . ."

I didn't hear the rest of Colt's sentence, if he finished it, because at that very moment a virtual fireball tore through Paula's apartment, sending her front door flying through the air. The explosion was so loud and intense, I was sure my ear drums had burst. And I was fairly sure I had screamed, but I didn't hear that either. I know I opened my mouth very wide and that my throat hurt after the dust settled.

"Holy cow," I roared. "Has this ever happened to you before?" I looked at Colt whose white-as-a-ghost face gave me my answer.

Forgetting the cold, I somehow managed to find my cell phone and dialed 911 with shaky-from-fright fingers.

"911, what's your emergency?"

"An apartment just exploded into a million pieces. Master Kyo and Paula were in there. Her name isn't Parra, it's Paula. Paula . . . Paula . . . Colt, what's her last name?" I wasn't being very coherent.

"Ma'am, calm down. Please, tell me your location."

"Rustic Woods."

"Where in Rustic Woods?"

That was a good question. Where was I? Colt had driven. I stepped out of the car and looked around. We were at the far end of the apartment complex parking lot. Traffic was whizzing past us on Rustic Woods Parkway to our left, and on the other side was Unified Bank, but I couldn't read the street number.

"Do you know the Unified Bank on Rustic Woods Parkway?" I asked.

"Ma'am, are you at the Colonial Arms Apartments on Purple Beech Tree Way?"

I scanned the area again and finally located a sign: Colonial Arms Apartments.

"Yes, yes I am."

"We've just taken a call from that location. Emergency vehicles are on their way. Are you hurt, Ma'am?"

"I'm a little shaken up."

"But are you hurt?"

"No."

"Then please stay where you are so police can take your statement on what you observed."

"Okay. I can do that. Um . . . could you do me a favor?"

"Ma'am?"

"Would you be able to contact the FBI and ask for agent Howard Marr? I'd like him to know I'm here so he can worry about me. See, we're sort of separated right now and . . ."

"Ma'am, we don't contact the FBI or estranged husbands." The phone clicked and my 911 friend was gone.

***

Ten minutes later, four fire trucks worked to put out the explosion-related fire that swept through the apartment building while EMTs tended a few injured. Two police helicopters circled above our heads.

Colt and I stood, leaning against his car, waiting for Officer Williams to return and take our statements. He had introduced himself, requested that we stay, and then moved off somewhere else. The air had warmed only slightly, but we were in the sun now, so I was slightly more comfortable.

"So, do you think the husband did this?"

Colt shook his head. "Not likely. And we don't know it was a bomb. Could have been a gas leak."

"Well, I never wanted to see Master Kyo die, but let me say this: Karma's a bitch."

"What do you mean?"

"He was a Korean Hitler, that man. He loved seeing me writhe in pain."

"Maybe you did this?" He flashed a playful, smirking smile.

"Yeah, right. Like I knew before we came here today, that Master Kyo was having an affair with Parra and was going to waltz into their secret love shack."

"Paula."

"Right."

"And we don't know they were having an affair."

"Right."

We were quiet for a while, but the activity around us continued at high volume. I thought about Paula and Master Kyo. Toasted in the prime of their life. What a horrible way to go.

I turned around and looked at the apartments behind us. The complex was several buildings deep with garden-style apartments. Each building was two stories high, with the front of the apartments opening onto a railed walkway. At the back, each apartment had a set of French doors opening onto a private balcony. They were okay as apartments go, but I wondered why they didn't choose something farther from their own homes – somewhere people would be less likely to know or recognize them.

My body tensed when I heard a familiar voice.

"Well, isn't this a cozy little scene." The voice was Howard's. The voice wasn't happy.

I chose not to turn around, but Colt, always the jovial fellow, jumped up and decided to play.

"Hey, Howie! Good to see you, roomie. Here on official business or just dropping by for a little afternoon delight with the Mrs.?"

A moment of silence indicated that Howard wasn't about to address that question directly. My neck was strained trying to keep my head turned, so mostly to avoid a visit to the chiropractor, I rotated it back.

Now, first off, I need to explain that my husband, Howard looks very much like George Clooney. It's true. It's not just my fantasy. Everyone says so. A little more gray, a little less chin. Maybe an inch or two taller. But he definitely looks like George Clooney. Lucky me, I know.

But as lucky as that is, there are drawbacks. For instance, most people don't know why I won't let my very handsome husband move back into our house. He's a good guy, they say. He's paid his dues, they say. Okay, mostly Howard says these things, but my friends say them as well.

Truth of the matter is, I would love for him to move back, but I want to bring some romance back into our marriage. I want him to date me and woo me. Romance me. Earn his way back.

See, he lied to me for our whole marriage about his line of work. I thought he was an engineer for a consulting firm, when in fact he was an agent for the FBI. And his real name wasn't Howard Marr, but Sammy Donato, and his father was whacked by a mafioso named Tito Buttaro. Another long story. Same book.

So, anyway, to make a long story longer – every time I see Howard, I'm torn between wanting to shoot him, and wanting to tear his clothes off and do wild and nasty things to him.

Thankfully, there were too many people around at that moment to allow me to perform either action, so I sheepishly stood up and faced his certain, squinty-eyed, I don't-approve-of-this expression. I felt like a teenager who'd been caught sneaking out of the house to smoke cigarettes.

"Hi, Honey!" I said, all happy and innocent-like.

"Barb, what are you doing here? Please tell me you weren't on a job with Colt."

"Okay, I won't tell you that I was on a job with Colt."

"Were you?"

"You just told me not to tell you that."

"Jesus!"

"Well then, don't ask questions if you don't want to hear the answers. Why are you here? The 911 operator told me they don't call the FBI."

"What?"

"Nothing."

"The FBI has business here. Don't tell me you witnessed this explosion."

"Okay, we didn't witness this explosion."

"You did. Damn it, Barb!"

"Geez, How-man, don't you talk to me anymore? I'm feeling a little left out here."

Howard glared Colt down and stuck a finger in his face. "I'll talk to you about this later. Problem is, right now I've got business to handle, and you both might be a part of that. Christ! I'll be right back." And Howard stalked off to talk to a hovering trio of policemen.

"He's not happy."

"Yeah, you're not putting out. He's sexually frustrated."

"Oh, shut up! Why did you drag me into this?"

"We're not going to have THAT conversation again, are we?"

As Howard stood there, his hands in his pockets, head nodding, surveying the area, I pondered his reason for being there. After his years of lying about his job with the FBI, truth had become an obvious necessity between us. At least, as much truth as he could provide. The FBI didn't allow him to reveal all things about his job these days, but he was able to tell me that he had most recently been assigned to the National Gang Task Force located at National Headquarters.

Why would the National Gang Task Force be interested in an explosion that had leveled Paula what's-her-name's apartment when she was meeting Master Kyo for a lunch-time quickie?

Something else was nagging at me. Something I had observed between Paula, Master Kyo, and of all people – my mother. She had convinced me that Tae Kwon Do would be the thing for me – get me in shape and teach me to protect myself in dangerous situations. I'm not sure I'd gotten in shape, but certainly I was always in so much pain, that whenever anyone came near me, I was likely to kill them. If that's what you call protection.

In any event, one day I'd mustered up the nerve to stop by Master Kyo's studio at a time when he wasn't having classes. My mission: to quit Tae Kwon Do. I'd had enough. The pain was too extreme. I had kids and a life – I didn't have time to soak my weary body in Epsom salts three times a week after an hour of cruel and unusual punishment to my aging body. It was time to end the misery.

However, when I'd walked in, he wasn't alone – he was in his office with Paula, my mother, and two young girls. They looked to be about my daughter Cassie's age – fourteen, maybe fifteen at the most. They were crying, and speaking in Spanish, which my mother seemed to be translating for Paula and Master Kyo. I hadn't even known my mother could speak Spanish. Of course she has a black belt in Tae Kwon Do, runs marathons, and claims to have gotten drunk with Ernest Hemingway, so I don't know why I should doubt that she could speak not only Spanish, but probably also Russian, Swahili and Urdu to boot.

While I pondered on that strange encounter at Master Kyo's, I saw a female figure walking along the path that parallels Rustic Woods Parkway. Not necessarily something that should catch my eye as suspicious, with two exceptions. Number one: the woman wasn't rubber necking at the disaster scene. Not a bit. Didn't crane her neck to look once. Half the cars on Rustic Woods Parkway had stopped in the middle of the road to watch the carnage unfold, but not this woman. Walking along like she didn't have a care in the world. Too odd.

Number two, and more important than number one: The woman was huge. Not fat, but extraordinarily tall, and freakishly big boned. To be blunt – a woman of colossal size. She was walking away from us, so I only saw her back, but that's all I needed to see to know that the woman was my own mother.

Damn!

Of course, the other problem with this little scenario is that my mother has an uncanny ability to sniff out my whereabouts from over one thousand miles away, so the fact that she was walking away from me and this mess meant one thing. She had something to hide.

I elbowed Colt.

"Psst. Don't be too obvious, but look over there at that woman."

"What woman?"

"On the path." I pointed down low with my index finger as discreetly as I could. "Don't let Howard see you looking."

Colt looked out of the corner of his eyes, one way toward the path, then back to me and whispered.

"Is that who I think it is?"

"I'm pretty sure it's not big foot. And with feet that big – if it's not big foot . . ."

"It's your mother."

"Do you think Howard has seen her yet?"

Colt shot a glance at Howard, who looked back in our direction. I froze. He yelled across from his huddle of law enforcement buddies. "You two stay right there – I'll be back in ten minutes. I need to talk to you both."

I gave a nod and a whatever-you-say-honey smile. Colt waved a terse, but cool half-wave indicating manly understanding – the way manly men do – and then Howard moved off in the opposite direction with two uniformed policemen.

"Okay, coast is clear, let's go," I said.

"What's up?"

"I don't know, but my mother's up to it."

"What are you talking about?"

"Just follow me. I may need your expertise."

Luckily, just to our left was a small cluster of evergreen trees that stood between us, and the parkway. It was an odd grouping of trees that didn't seem to be there either for privacy or aesthetic purposes, but it served our needs at the moment. I snuck behind the small grove motioning Colt to follow, which he did.

"Do you have a plan?" he asked.

"Yes."

"What is it?"

"To formulate a plan."

Once safely behind the trees, I started moving down the path. Parkway traffic crept at a snail's pace next to us and ahead, my mother's hulking frame moved steadily away. She was carrying a plastic grocery bag filled nearly to capacity.

"Why are you so concerned about your mother, anyway?"

"Last time I saw her, she was with Paula and Master Kyo. Ordinarily she'd be all over this scene – probably telling the police how to do their job. I don't trust her – she's up to something."

"Your mother scares me."

"Really? You're the only person I know who doesn't cower around her."

"It's a façade. I'm smiling on the outside, quaking on the inside."

I peeked back to assess the crime scene and determine our ability to make a run for it without being noticed. I didn't see Howard. More official cars had arrived. They were unmarked. Probably FBI. The fire in the apartment had been put out, and firemen looked like they were in heavy discussion about what to do next. I figured now was as good a time as any.

"Okay – run!"

"No," said Colt pulling me back. "Don't run. That will attract attention. Walk fast. Look like you belong on the path. PI trick."

We took off at a fast walking clip.

"How do you look like you belong on the path?"

"It takes a lot of practice."

Ahead of us, my mother took a sharp and unexpected turn to the right into one of my favorite small shopping plazas. I knew those shops well. When the weather turned frosty, I turned to Positively Polly's Coffee, Tea and Read. It was a cozy little bookstore with a coffee and tea bistro. I would also buy birthday cards and wrapping paper at Danielle's Cards and Gifts, order flowers for teacher appreciation day from Rustic Woods Fancy Floral, and occasionally get a sandwich at Parkway Panache.

We quickened our pace to a slow jog. We were well past the apartment complex by that time, so we thought we were safe.

A plaza sign and another set of trees obscured my view. I was afraid I had lost her, but luckily I caught sight of her again as she moved onto the sidewalk in front of a vacant shop next to Rustic Woods Fancy Floral. The windows were covered from the inside with white paper and a posted sign read: Space For Rent.

My mother put the bag down and pulled something out of the purse slung over her left shoulder. Next thing I knew, she was slipping a key into the lock and walking into the vacant shop. Grabbing my head with both of my hands, I worked to suppress a growing headache. My mother had a way of giving me headaches.

"Why does your mother have keys to that place?" Colt asked.

"No idea." The headache throbbed mercilessly.

"Let's go see."

"Do we have to?" I whined.

"You started this. Besides, my only job went up in smoke an hour ago, so I have nothing better to do."

"Fine." True, I had started it, but I was chickening out. My mother has a way of bringing out the cowardly fowl in me.

Colt and I scooted across the parking lot, moving inconspicuously just to the side of the large plate glass windows of the vacant shop. Trying to peek inside was difficult since the windows were mostly covered. I had about one inch of clear glass which allowed me to see two panted legs from the shin down and feet wearing loafers. They looked like women's loafers – small feet, so I knew they weren't my mother's. The legs moved back and forth like the person owning them was pacing.

My headache increased with the squinting required to peep through the small opening. I was getting colder and grumpier by the minute as a sharp, brisk wind screamed past me.

Finally, I'd had enough. With a loud grunt, I grabbed the door and gave it a tug. It didn't budge. My mother had locked it behind her. Grabbing the silver door handle with both hands, I shook the locked door violently and screamed.

"Mother! Let me in! I know you're in there!"

"Way to be discreet there, Curly."

Ignoring Colt's remark, I started pounding on the door. "Mother! I want in this minute. I'm cold and tired, and now the aroma from Parkway Panache is making me hungry. I'm not happy here! Let me in!"

By now, passersby were staring at me and whispering to each other. Colt smiled. Just before I was about to give the door another jerk, the dead bolt snapped back and the door opened just wide enough to allow my mother's decidedly large and perfectly coifed head to emerge. She saw Colt first.

"Well, well. Colt Baron. What are you doing here?" She was playing innocent. My mother doesn't play innocent very well.

"Mother! What is going on here?" I was seething.

"Oh, Barbara. I didn't see you there. Do you think you could come back later, dear? I'm a little busy right now."

"You're kidding me."

"No. Not kidding. Very serious. Opening a business is very serious work you know. No time for idle banter."

She tried to pull her head back into the store, but I stopped her.

"A business? What business?"

"A sandwich shop."

"Mom – Parkway Panache is right next door. Why would you open a sandwich shop here?"

"Their bread is too stale and their sandwich names aren't very original. I can do better. Okay. Enough talk. Back to work . . ."

There was no way I was letting her close that door. "Not so fast – let me see this place." And with one swift pull, the door was wide open and I was marching in past my mother only to come face-to-face with the two people I'd thought had bit the dust back at the Colonial Arms.

"Master Kyo!" I couldn't believe my eyes. "Paula. You're not dead."

Colt had followed me inside. "Interesting twist."

"If nothing else," said Paula to my mother, "you've raised an observant daughter. At least she's saying my name right, for once."

"Right," I said. "Sorry about that."

"You not here!" Master Kyo shouted.

"I may not want to be here, but like the lady said, I am observant, and I am definitely here. The question is, *how* are you here?"

"No! You not here!" He was limping in circles around the very empty space and waving his hands wildly in the air over his head. For a short little guy he sure could whip up some wind.

"Ruin everything! Away! Away!"

"He's saying you shouldn't be here," Paula translated.

"We shouldn't be here?" I yelled. "We just watched your secret love hideaway blow up like a Roman candle on the Fourth of July, with you supposedly in it, so I wouldn't be pointing fingers right now."

"Love hideaway? What are you talking about?"

"Your apartment. We know about it. Your husband knows about it."

"Well, it's not a love hideaway for crying out loud. And the explosion wasn't our fault."

"We on a missing!" screeched Kyo.

Colt had been assessing the space. "Whose fault was it?"

Paula rubbed her temples. "They knew about our set-up, so we snuck the girls out fast, late last night. We came back today to pack up their things and our supplies, when Master Kyo saw something that looked like bomb on a timer behind the couch. It was them. Had to be."

Set-up? Girls? And who were "They"? I was bordering on a major breakdown. "Mother, what have you gotten yourself into?"

"We on a missing!" Kyo shrieked again.

"We were watching that apartment all morning," said Colt. "You both went in but never came out before that explosion tore the place apart."

"We jumped out the back balcony. Why do you think he's limping?"

"Missing! Missing! Eeet a missing!"

This Korean midget of a dictator was starting to ruffle my already irritated feathers. "What is he saying?"

"Barbara," interrupted my mother. "You need to understand. We're doing some very important humanitarian work here. He's saying we're on a mission. This is already very dangerous – if they find out you're connected to the FBI, it could make things much worse."

There was that word again. "They?" I asked. Who's 'they'?"

Before my mother could answer, a young girl with long dark hair came out of a back room. She was followed by two more girls, one of them helping the other who was bent over and holding her very large stomach. I was pretty sure two of them were the girls I had seen in Master Kyo's office over a week ago.

"Scuze me, missus. Maria very sick. She need help – maybe hospital." The young girl who must have been Maria screamed out in pain.

"Uh oh," said Colt, backing up. "I don't know nothin' 'bout birthin' no babies."

"Oh Lord," cried Paula, "this just keeps getting worse by the minute. What are we going to do?" Paula helped the young laboring girl to the floor against a wall.

"Mother, who are these girls?"

"They're slaves, Barbara. Slaves."

"What?"

Another pain-filled scream from Maria was followed by the whooshing sound of the shop door opening. Two young men, probably not much older than the three young girls, stepped inside, hands tucked suspiciously into their hooded jacket pockets. Their black hair matched their menacing black eyes. Black peach fuzz topped their lips. Both sported red bandanas tied around their left thigh. I didn't think it was a fashion statement.

The tallest and scariest looking of the two spoke with an eerie sense of calm to one of the girls. The words were Spanish. She wasn't so calm as she listened. Her eyes darted from him to my mother and then to Master Kyo, then back again to the intimidating duo. Finally she replied, again in Spanish.

My hands had gone clammy and my legs felt like limp egg noodles. I didn't know exactly what was going on, but I knew I should be scared. Colt kept looking out of the corner of one eye, while also assessing the situation with our two visitors, who had not moved from their position in front of the door.

More undecipherable Spanish dialogue exchanged between the two, while poor Maria and the other young girl wept softly.

"Sofia, what he say?" asked Master Kyo.

The girl had tears in her eyes. "He says we must go with him. They will kill us all if we do not go now."

Master Kyo erupted again, his arms waving about in the air, punctuating his barely understandable words.

"No! No! Dis not white! I not let happen!"

Young man number two, who had been silent up till now, remained so while he pulled a very large and threatening handgun out of his pocket to let Master Kyo know that silence was probably a good thing. Master Kyo got the point and shut up quick like.

Poor Paula looked like she was going to be sick. I wasn't feeling too whippy myself.

"Sofia – you can't go," said my mother.

"Mom, maybe they should work this out amongst themselves. It seems like a domestic dispute sort of thing here."

"Barbara! You don't understand. These girls are slaves. Forced prostitutes – they were kidnapped from their families when they were no older than Bethany and brought here to make money for these scum hoodlums. Have you ever heard of the gang, MS 13? Eventually they'll just kill these girls when they don't serve their needs anymore."

Now I felt like I was going to be sick. My Bethany was only ten. Not only had I heard of MS 13, but suddenly I realized why Howard was at the scene of the explosion.

My mother had worked herself into a frenzy and went off like a rabid dog on the two gang members, screaming a slew of Spanish words at them. I had no idea what she was saying, but I was fairly sure she wasn't reminiscing about her days as a showgirl in Vegas.

While she knows how to irritate the hell out of me, she is my mother, and my first instinct was to protect her. As I moved in her direction, Peach Fuzz Number One grabbed me by the neck and shoved my face into the glass pane in front of me.

With my face squished against the window, one eye had a perfect view through a thin amount of unobscured glass. Just on the other side stood my handsome Howard. Certainly, I thought, he'd brought half the FBI with him. The problem was, had they come in time? Actually, the bigger problem was, would I pass out while this pumped-up pimp choked the air out of me? The room started to spin while screams filled the air and glimpses of Master Kyo, my mother and Colt shot in and out of my blurred peripheral vision.

Somehow, I managed to grab hold of two fingers that were wrapped around my neck, pulling them away so that more air could make it through my trachea. Where was Howard with the troops? Didn't he hear the screaming?

I became more aware of some sort of wrestling match, and realized it was Master Kyo going all Korean crazy on Peach Fuzz Number Two. Legs and arms were flying at lightning speeds. I saw the gun fly through the air.

Meanwhile, if I wanted to maintain consciousness, I had to do something. My Tae Kwon Do skills had been mediocre at best, but now was not the time to question ability. Now was the time to do or be done.

With all of the awareness I could gather and all of the strength I could muster, I grabbed, pulled and kicked. I kicked like I'd never kicked before. Peach Fuzz Number One went down fast, grabbing his crotch the whole way down. Turned out my far-flung foot had landed hard and square on the grisly gang member's gonads. Ouch.

Finally able to breathe, I regained my balance and looked up to see what was happening around me. A quick check told me all I needed to know: Master Kyo and Peach Fuzz Number Two were going at it, although it seemed PF was on the losing end of the battle. Colt was crawling for the gun which was half-way across the room on the floor. My mother and Paula were in the corner with Maria, who appeared to be in full blown labor.

Figuring I needed to get Howard and his crime-fighting friends in to stop the blood bath, I turned and pushed hard on the door, nearly falling out onto the sidewalk in front of the shop. There stood Howard to my left, still standing like I had seen through the window. What I hadn't seen at that time, however, and which was now in clear view, was the mammoth man standing behind him, gun trained on his head. A tattoo ran along the right side of his face and his red bandana was wrapped around his thick, bald head. The monstrous goon seemed very pleased with his catch, and through the shit-eating grin he wore on his face, I could tell he was missing both top front teeth.

What I also saw were the four Fairfax County police squad cars all poised in my direction, with uniformed officers next to them, aiming their own firearms squarely at Howard and his toothless shadow.

Instinctively, I put my arms in the air, even though I was innocent of any wrongdoing.

"Howard?"

"Barb. Don't move."

"Am I allowed to pee my pants?"

"Can't laugh right now."

"Who's your friend?"

"Meet Julio Jimenez."

"He looks like a killer."

"He is."

"Are we going to die?"

"Not if I can help it."

"You have a plan?"

"Nope."

"That's encouraging."

"Barb."

"Yeah?"

"I – "

Howard couldn't finish his sentence. He was interrupted by Peach Fuzz Number One, who had evidently recovered from my powerful punch to his privates. Peach Fuzz came flying through the door, attacking me from behind.

"I'll kill you, beetch!" he screamed, grabbing at my neck again. Luckily he was still off kilter, and so toppled and landed on his face, only knocking me over, but on my way down I heard the deafening pow, pow, pow of gunfire. Then another, and then another. I had no idea where they were coming from. Was Howard dead?

I tried to get up, but Peach Fuzz was still on a mission to end my life. He had crawled up on top of me and I could feel his hot guacamole breath in my face.

"You're mine, beetch," he said, pulling my hair and scratching my cheek with a shiny silver six-inch blade. He moved the blade quickly to my throat.

It was like one of those awful dreams where you want to scream – you have to scream – but you can't. You open your mouth, and no sound comes out. People were all around me, but I had no idea if I was going to live or die.

Suddenly, I realized dying wasn't an option. I had three girls to raise. There was no way in hell I was going to die and let someone tell those girls that their mom had been too weak to save her own life. What kind of mother would I be?

Without another thought, I dug my teeth, all twenty-four of them, into his bad-ass arm like a hungry piranha. He screamed, dropped the blade and rolled off of me. While I was rolling in the opposite direction, I heard another pop. When I looked over, Peach Fuzz Number One was limp and bleeding.

A familiar voice in my ear said, "He was going for the knife again. I had to do it." The familiar voice was Howard's. The familiar voice made me very happy.

That night, the news reported that there had been a shooting at a small shopping plaza in Rustic Woods, Virginia. Three men had been fatally shot, and the assailants were still at large. The Fairfax County Police could not confirm if it was gang related, but the FBI's National Gang Task Force had been called on the scene to review the situation. Interestingly, there was no mention of the apartment explosion.

Maria made it to the hospital just in time to give birth to a healthy baby girl who she named Paula Diane. The other two girls, Sofia and Amelia were taken to a women's shelter. Howard assured me they would be cared for and kept under police protection until their families were found and could be notified that their daughters were alive and well.

The next morning, Howard came by the house after a long night of tying up loose ends and writing reports. Deep circles under his eyes told me he'd barely slept, if at all. I poured him a cup of coffee and we sat quietly, enjoying the married couple ritual.

"So, you gonna let me move back in, now that I've saved your life?"

"Maybe. You have to tell me something first."

"What?"

"How did you find us in that shop?"

"I had you followed, of course."

"You don't trust me?"

"I don't trust Colt."

"He's your roommate."

"That's why he's my roommate. I can keep tabs on him. He's still in love with you, you know."

"He's harmless. He's our friend."

Howard silently stared at his coffee, not offering a reply.

"Barb?"

"Yeah?"

"I –"

"Knock, knock! Hello! Anyone home?" It was my mother. The knock, knock was rhetorical. She always barged in uninvited and unannounced.

Howard rolled his eyes. He was not my mother's favorite person, and the lack of affinity was mutual.

I wanted to hear what Howard had to say. "What?"

"Nothing, I'll tell you later."

"There you are," stated my mother, as if she seriously didn't think she'd find us. "Coffee? Do you mind if I have some?" Rhetorical again. She was already pouring. "It's colder than a witch's heart out there. Barbara dear, how are you? I've been so worried about you. Look at that cut on your face!"

"I'm fine, mom. It will heal. You didn't say hello to Howard."

"Hello, Howard."

"Diane."

"How are things at the Bureau?"

"We've got things under control, Diane – no thanks to you. You're on our radar now."

"I'm on everyone's radar. Did I ever tell you that I once turned down a job with the CIA?"

Howard rolled his eyes again.

"Those girls needed our help, Howard Marr. You and your boys don't get the job done. And there's more of them out there. Hundreds, maybe thousands, of these poor girls. Who cares about them? Who's going to get the job done and sweep the streets of the slime who enslave those poor souls?"

"Diane, your intentions were good, but you almost got them, yourself, and your daughter killed yesterday. Leave the street sweeping to those of us who are trained to handle these things, okay?"

My mother sniffed, took a quick sip of her coffee, and then setting the cup down, made a new declaration.

"Well, I'm off. I have an appointment with Senator Thomas today. I'm joining her campaign – I'll be her speech writer."

"Since when are you a speech writer?"

"I told you before, I've written several books, including two memoirs. I plan to publish them someday." She looked at her watch. "I'm late!" And in her usual Endora-from-Bewitched manner, she was gone as quickly as she had appeared.

"Is what she said true?"

"About turning down a job with the CIA?"

"About more girls out there – forced prostitution."

Howard nodded. "It is. These gangs aren't pretty and they aren't nice. Drug running, human trafficking – it's their business. It's how they make a living."

"It's gross."

Howard nodded again.

"I never hear about this on the news. You'd think they'd be all over stories on like this."

"People care about their retirement funds and stock market portfolios. It's easier to confront. Girls being kidnapped and sold into slavery – not so easy to confront. Easier to ignore it, or pretend it's someone else's problem."

"It's gross."

"You said that already."

"Because it's true."

"We're doing what we can. I promise." He stood up, kissed me on the head, and looked me in the eyes.

"I have to go too – people to meet with, slime to lock up. The usual. Can I take you out to dinner tonight?"

"I thought you'd never ask. I'll have to check with my husband, though," I smiled as I followed him.

"I don't think he'll mind."

The doorbell rang just before Howard reached the door.

"Hmm, wonder who that is?"

I spied a man from Rustic Woods Fancy Floral standing outside the open door.

"These might be for you," Howard said with a sneaky smile on his face, as he walked past the man who holding the suspiciously long, ribboned box.

After signing and thanking Joe the Floral Man, I ripped open the box – a dozen purple roses – my favorite color. The card read: *Life is too short. Let the romance begin. I love you. Howard.*

"The Recollections of Rosabelle Raines"

This short story was originally published in the mystery anthology,
Chesapeake Crimes: They Had it Comin'

Rosabelle Raines had lived at least a thousand lives, and much to her dismay, she could recall them all.

Lying on the cold, winter ground, Rosabelle rubbed her aching eyes while she recovered from the most recent incident. Some wisps of her fine, ebony hair had slipped from their silk netting, falling over her face.

"Rosa," whispered her sister, Flora. "Are you with me?"

Drained of energy, Rosabelle moaned, but would be unable to speak for a minute or more.

"Does this happen often?" The man she heard speaking appeared as a blur at the end of her tunneled vision. He seemed to hover miles away, but in reality, his warm face was nearly touching hers. She could smell his breath – a touch of ale, she thought, and possibly some corned beef. She detested corned beef.

"She . . . she has . . . fainting spells." Flora offered a worried, tentative explanation. Weaker in spirit than Rosabelle, she was badly affected by her sister's spells. They gave Flora such distress that she would suffer stomach maladies for many days after.

"We should get her to a doctor," the man urged.

"No!" Rosabelle shouted, her voice returning just in time. Rosabelle found herself sitting upright, and the man responsible for her condition was no longer a distant blur. Pleasing to her eyes, he was fair of skin and possessed a head of enviously thick hair the color of summer wheat. In his left hand he clutched a newspaper and a stovepipe hat made of a fine silk that belied his humble station. Perhaps the hat was a tribute to the late President Lincoln. Rosabelle might not care for his corned beef breath, but she would consider a person of good spirit if he revered a man the likes of Mr. Lincoln. Not a popular sentiment for a woman from the South, Rosabelle knew, but she did not often subscribe to opinions just because they were popular.

"I have no need for a doctor, sir. A brisk walk in the fresh air and some tea at our destination will be the only medicine I need." She brushed a strand of hair out of her eyes. "Flora, could you help me to my feet please?" Rosabelle placed a hand in the shallow snow to give her some leverage, while holding the other up for her sister's assistance.

"Here, let me help." Eli Witherspoon, the young man who had touched Rosabelle's hand by way of introduction just moments earlier, was about to touch her again by placing his own hand under her back as support in her attempt to stand.

Signaling him to keep his distance, Rosabelle rebuffed his offer promptly. "No! You have done enough." Stuttering a moment on her words, she quickly corrected herself. "What I mean to say is you are too kind. Truly, sir, your assistance is unnecessary. We have a system, my sister and I." With minor struggle, Rosabelle was on her feet. She quickly tucked the wayward strands back into her snood, attempting to regain some appearance of dignity. "See? I am upright." Rosabelle gave a slight curtsy to Mr. Witherspoon while brushing snow from her sapphire velvet cape, then placed her hands back in her muff for warmth. Only then did she recognize the newspaper the young man held.

"Interesting article, is it not?" Rosabelle asked.

He looked at the paper with an odd expression, as if it had materialized out of nowhere. "Ah. Well . . ." He cleared his throat. "I have not read this paper yet." He fidgeted in a nervous manner, shoving the paper under his arm.

"You should!" Flora exclaimed, her eyes brightening. "Rosa and I read it earlier today – a fascinating story about a lady spy! What was her name, Rosa?"

"Abigail. Abigail Dawes," Rosabelle answered, studying the distracted Mr. Witherspoon intently.

"That is the name!" Flora said. "A lady spy for the South. Evidently she is a master of disguise. It is very intriguing. She escaped from jail some three weeks ago now. Gives me goose pimples all over my arms."

Mr. Witherspoon pulled a watch from his breast pocket to check the time. "That . . . is . . . yes. Interesting. Well, excuse me for my abruptness, but . . ."

"No." Rosabelle put her hand up as if to stop his words mid-air. "Excuse us, sir. Come, Flora, we will be late for our engagement with the Waters family."

Rosabelle rushed away, her long hooped skirt pushing the snow along like a plow, while Flora, trailing desperately behind her, looked back at Eli Witherspoon, giving him an apologetic smile.

Flora's interest in Mr. Witherspoon was not lost on Rosabelle, but she did not have time to be concerned with such trivial matters. Not since her recollection.

"Rosa," Flora wheezed, finally reaching her sister. "You were so rude to Mr. Witherspoon."

"Me, rude? Did you see how strangely he was behaving?"

"Maybe you intimidated him. You have that effect on people. Oh! I very much wanted to speak with him longer."

"Sister," Rosabelle said, stopping abruptly and pointing down the road from where they had come. "Look. Your Mr. Witherspoon has disappeared into thin air." Indeed there was no sign of the man.

Rosabelle continued on. "And did you hear him say he had not yet read the newspaper?"

"Well—"

"Yet it was crinkled and worn and turned to the Abigail Dawes article several pages in."

"But—"

"Flora, something is afoot with that man, and before the day is done, he will either kill or be killed. If you have an interest in this Mr. Eli Witherspoon, come help devise a way to determine which it will be. Hopefully we can stop this crime before it occurs."

Full of vigor and intention, Rosabelle turned on her heel and quickly crossed King Street just as a horse and buggy passed. Flora jogged to catch up.

"These dreams of yours!" Flora panted as she trotted closely behind her sister, her blonde locks bouncing. "Why must you have them? Mr. Witherspoon seems to be gentle and kind. Surely you are wrong."

"Flora," Rosabelle corrected, blue eyes flashing. "I have told you before – these are not dreams. They are recollections. Memories of my other lives."

"How could you possibly know this?"

"How do I know the air is free to breathe? How do I know to smile when I see snow fall from the sky or to cry when a baby dies? I just know. I know."

"Bah! Other lives. You speak such blasphemy! We live only one life on this Earth, then, God willing, an eternity with Him. How can you think otherwise?" Flora pressed her hand to her bodice. "Dear, my stomach turns. I am feeling ill."

"Remember before the war, when Father entertained those importers from Japan? They called themselves Buddhists – they believe we maintain a cycle on Earth of birth, life, death, and then re-birth. It is not an uncommon belief, this idea that we are reborn to new bodies after we die. Much of the world believes the same."

"Pagans!" Flora was fanning herself.

"Flora, you don't even know what a pagan is," Rosabelle responded, rolling her eyes. She was easily annoyed by her sister's fears. Flora did not fare well with anything outside of the ordinary nor expected.

"Well, I know the people of this town would consider you a witch and have you burned at the stake," Flora huffed, obviously proud of her foreboding comment.

"I should hope the day of witch burning is past us, but you speak correctly regarding local sentiment. If word of this got out, I could be shunned or, even worse, put in an asylum for the ill of mind."

Flora shook her head. "It scares me so, Rosa."

"Listen to me – we keep this secret between us, and no one will suffer. Now tell me," she said, changing the subject, "when did you meet Mr. Witherspoon?"

"Last Sunday at church. You would know that if you had been there."

"I was there."

"Inside God's house, not outside, contemplating your many wild and sinful lives."

Exasperated, Rosabelle heaved a healthy sigh. Flora could be so trying. "Let us stay with the topic at hand, shall we? Who introduced you?"

"Amelia Patton," her sister replied. "Eli Witherspoon is her cousin, come to Alexandria to work at her father's shipping company. He studied at the University of Virginia," Flora stated with a hint of awe in her voice.

Rosabelle stopped walking for a moment. "Amelia Patton? Is he living in the Patton home?"

"I think so. Why?"

Ignoring Flora's question, Rosabelle resumed her determined trek. "About my recollection – it began when Mr. Witherspoon touched my hand. I saw two men. Both wore tattered garb made of wool. Their hair was long and unkempt, with some strands in braids; their faces bearded. One man was fair-haired and pale while the other had dark hair and eyes black like onyx. This darker man was tending a field of some sort, but it was on a hill. The fair-haired man rode up on a horse and dismounted. They talked and shook hands. When the dark man turned back to continue his work, the fair man drew a large knife and stabbed him in the back." Rosabelle shivered with the memory.

"Rosa, I don't understand how you connect your dream – your recollection – with Mr. Witherspoon. Are you saying the fair man is Eli Witherspoon?"

Rosabelle shook her head. "I am not sure. What I do know is this: every time I have a recollection, the person who touched me is involved in an incident almost identical to the recollection."

The strange episodes began nearly a year earlier, just after their mother passed on. Since their father had died before her while fighting for the South, they had become orphans of sorts, even though Rosabelle was twenty and Flora, eighteen. Without husbands to care for them, they were forced to move from Norfolk to Alexandria to live with their Aunt Martha and Uncle Ephraim. Even though Martha and Ephraim Raines had been warm and inviting in every way possible, losing both of their parents and leaving the only home they had ever known proved tragically painful for both girls. It was during that emotional time that Rosabelle experienced her first recollection.

They always occurred in the same way. A person would touch her, by way of introduction, possibly, or just in passing. At that moment, Rosabelle would find herself in another world, watching a scene unfold before her. When Mrs. Kincaid put her hands on Rosabelle's shoulder during a quilting party, for example, she had seen a woman drown in the middle of the sea while a ship went down in flames nearby. Later that day, Mrs. Kincaid drowned in the Potomac when she slipped off a pier and was swept away by the heavy current.

Each time Rosabelle had a recollection, she would relay the story to Flora with amazing detail. Within a day's time, a similar event would always occur, and always involving the person who had touched Rosabelle, initiating the memory.

The latest recollection involved four-year-old Edwin Hutchins. Rosabelle had agreed to care for him while his mother walked to market for some fish. Full of a little boy's energy, his blond curls bounced when he bounced. He took Rosabelle's hand with his own chubby little fingers and smiled up at her. Immediately Rosabelle was beneath a tree dressed in the most exquisite finery, mounted on a spectacular steed. An armored man rode past her, but she paid little attention to him. Instead she was calling a name. William. She was calling and calling, and she felt fear. Then a young boy's voice rang out. It came from above her. She looked into the tree. In its highest branches was a beautiful boy with red hair and blue eyes who smiled down at her. He moved as if to make his way down the branches, but his foot slipped. Before she could hear the scream from her own mouth, he was on the ground, mangled. Dead.

Still unaccustomed to her recollections, and not convinced that the related incidents weren't just coincidental, Rosabelle neglected any action. She told Flora, but she did not say a word of her vision to poor Edwin's mother, who found her son the next day in a mangled heap on the ground beneath their tall oak tree.

Gift or curse, Rosabelle no longer cared. She had vowed that day never to dismiss a recollection again. She would stop this eventual murder. The problem was, she had no idea if the handsome Eli Witherspoon would be the murderer or his victim.

***

Rosabelle turned the corner to a quieter street lined with tall, handsome brick homes.

"Rosa, you've turned on the wrong street." Flora pointed in the opposite direction. "The Waters family lives that way."

"They will have to wait. What we need is more information about Mr. Witherspoon."

"Where would we possibly find any such information?" Flora asked, losing her breath in a desperate attempt to keep pace with Rosabelle.

"Where else, but in a room full of women?" Rosabelle smiled while stopping in front of the finest of the brick townhouses, at 220 Prince Street.

Rosabelle climbed the five brick steps to the artfully carved walnut door, seized the brass, pineapple door knocker, and rapped smartly three times. By the time the door opened, Flora had made her way next to Rosabelle and the two of them were greeted by a small Negro woman who would not look directly at either of them.

"Good day, Miss." Rosabelle offered the young woman a friendly smile. "We are here for a meeting of the Alexandria Women's League. Please tell your mistress that Rosabelle and Flora Raines have arrived."

A large voice boomed from behind the servant, followed by the sudden appearance of the elaborately jeweled woman who belonged to the voice. Mrs. Harriet Franklin was large in body, personality, wealth, and reputation. Rooms seemed to shrink when she filled them. Her billowing, silk and lace skirt only accentuated her wide girth, and Rosabelle was certain Mrs. Franklin intended it exactly so. Mrs. Franklin loved the spotlight.

"Miss Raines!" Mrs. Franklin bellowed. "Such social graces are not necessary when addressing my Negroes," she laughed. "They may not be slaves any longer, but their station remains the same. What a surprise to see you. We thought you had another engagement."

"Yes, but your lovely neighbor and our esteemed friend, Miss Amelia Patton, convinced us we should change our plans. Is she here yet?"

"I'm afraid not. Any moment I should imagine, though. Lucy, take their capes and bonnets, then get back to help with the preparations. There is much to do; I will not stand for slacking today."

"Yes'm." The girl curtsied to her demeaning employer. Lucy took Flora's wrap and muff as they were handed to her, then reached for Rosabelle's. Rosabelle smiled again at the shy Lucy, who looked more toward the floor than toward Rosabelle while attempting to take charge of her overgarments. During the exchange, Rosabelle grazed Lucy's cold, dry hand. Before she could catch her breath, she was in another time. Looking around, she knew she having another recollection.

But there was something oddly familiar about this memory. She was crouched behind a massive bush that pricked her skin, and the air was cold and damp. She heard the sound of a horse's hooves on hard ground and a man calling another man's name. Crawling on hands and knees to peer around the bushes, Rosabelle gasped. It was the fair man on the horse and the dark man tending the fields. This was the same recollection as the one she experienced when introduced to Eli Witherspoon, with the exception that everything seemed enhanced a hundred fold. Sounds were clearer, colors brighter, and she felt . . . emotion.

She looked down at her own body. Dressed in peasant rags, Rosabelle had the hands of a small girl of eight or nine, maybe. She was breathing shallow, erratic gulps of air. She was afraid of this thin-skinned, blond man, but she did not know why. As before, the dark-haired man greeted his visitor, words were exchanged and hands were shook. Rosabelle's fear grew, knowing the end of this story and feeling hopeless to stop it. Once again, when the dark man turned around, the fair man drew his blade and sank it deep into the farmer's back. Rosabelle covered her eyes hard and screamed. When she opened her eyes, she was on the floor in the Franklin's foyer, with Mrs. Franklin waving a foul-smelling vial under her nose.

As usually happened after her recollections, Rosabelle was unable to speak. She would remain mute for a minute or two. Flora twittered on to the many women who had gathered around.

"She has these fainting spells. I am so sorry to be a burden like this, as is Rosa. So sorry. She will be fine. If someone can help me raise her from the floor . . ."

"The sofa in the parlor," Mrs. Franklin exclaimed. "She can recover there." Turning to one of the young women, she added, "Anna dear, fetch Dr. Gordon."

Rosabelle shook her head violently while scanning the room for Lucy.

"You are so kind, Mrs. Franklin," Flora said. "But Rosa does not want . . . I mean . . . she has already seen the doctor. These are just mild fainting spells due to . . . low nutrition, you see. A cup of tea and an orange or pear will bring her around just beautifully. Thank you. And some space, I should think, if you please."

With the aid of Marjorie Baker, one of the other guests, Flora successfully moved Rosabelle to the parlor sofa where she found her voice to thank Marjorie for her help and kindness.

"Of course, of course. Let us adjourn to the library – we will continue our meeting there – and leave Rosabelle and Flora some air." Mrs. Franklin herded the dozen women and their voluptuous hooped shirts out of the room, closing the tall double doors behind her.

Rosabelle had been rubbing her head more for the drama than for the purpose of relieving an ache, but once the doors closed, she grabbed Flora's arm.

"Sister! You will not believe what I just witnessed."

Flora tugged her arm away and pressed her index fingers to her own temples.

"Rosa, these dreams of yours – they come too often! They wear me down. Can you not control them?"

"No more than I can control the seasons. Flora, I need you now. Please, listen."

"Fine. What did you see this time?"

"It was the same recollection."

"The same as what?"

"Eli Witherspoon. When I touched Lucy's hand, I witnessed the entire murder again."

"Lucy? Who is Lucy?"

"Mrs. Franklin's maid."

"You mean the Negro girl?"

"Yes."

"I don't understand."

"Lucy must be one of the two men in my recollection. Lucy and Eli Witherspoon."

"Well," Flora sniffed. "That seems very odd."

Rosabelle fell back on the sofa laughing.

"What?" Flora asked.

"Is not all of this to be classified as odd, sister?"

Flora, who remained serious for just a moment, finally found the humor in it and laughed as well, which pleased Rosabelle. She desperately needed her sister to accept her condition, as she was the only person in whom Rosabelle could confide completely.

The two sisters sat smiling silently on the sofa for a moment, soaking in the absurdity of their new reality.

"Do you suppose then," Flora said finally, "that Lucy is going to murder Eli Witherspoon?"

"Or is he to murder her? That is precisely what I need to determine. This recollection was different. More detail, and I was acutely aware that I was a young girl. Do not ask me how I know this, but the dark man – he was my father. Also, I felt true fear when the other man rode up on his horse. Feeling fear when Lucy touched me – does this mean that Lucy is the murderer and Mr. Witherspoon the victim? I don't know. I just don't know.

"Do you suppose we should do something?" Flora asked.

"At the very least, for the moment, I would like to put my eyes on Lucy."

A loud rapping at the front door, followed by a flurry of activity and female chattering, compelled Rosabelle and Flora to leave their temporary sanctuary.

Opening the double doors of the parlor, they found that the women had not yet moved to the library. Instead, they were huddling around Mrs. Franklin who read aloud from a note in her hand.

"Miss Amelia Patton sends her regrets. She is ill and thus will be unable to attend today's meeting."

Mrs. Franklin put a hand to her heart. "Poor dear. She has not been looking well these last two days."

"I think she has worried herself sick," piped in Marjorie Baker, who stood next to Flora.

"Worried herself about what?" Rosabelle asked.

"That cousin of hers, Eli Witherspoon. Rumor has it he will be the next to die," Marjorie responded more quietly for deeper effect.

"It is true," clucked Mrs. Franklin in her strong, superior tone. "But I must say though, that the young man most likely brought it all upon himself with his questionable ways."

Rosabelle put two comforting hands on Flora's shoulders.

"What are you talking about?" Flora's voice trembled. "Who would want to kill Mr. Witherspoon?"

"The Southern Avenger, of course," Marjorie said.

"The Southern what?" Rosabelle asked, soaking in every bit of information thrown her way. It was a stroke of luck for her that this conversation should arise now. She could weed through truths and untruths later, but the current situation required her to take in everything.

"The Southern Avenger is what they are calling him. He's killed five men already. All of them Northern sympathizers and traitors who put slaves before the needs of the South. Rumor has it that Eli Witherspoon will be next."

"Why?" Rosabelle asked.

Mrs. Franklin lowered her voice and squinted her eyes. "He was a slave sympathizer during the war. He helped many escape from their owners."

Some of the women, obviously unaware of this rumor, grew wide-eyed and covered open mouths with their hands. Others, who must have been privy to the scandalous gossip, nodded knowingly yet disapprovingly.

One of those women was Anna Cameron. Seeing Rosabelle's confusion, Anna took great satisfaction in sharing her own prized information. Moving her face close to Rosabelle's, she whispered. "The word is that he loved a Negro girl who was killed transporting escaped slaves to the North during the war. Can you imagine? A man of fine, southern breeding keeping with Negroes? If you ask me, he has it coming."

"I think we should let God be the judge of that," Rosabelle said. "Unless the Lord has passed responsibility for judgment on to you, Anna." The room became as silent as a tomb. "Now, has anyone ever seen this Southern Avenger?"

The women looked around at each other, then many shook their heads.

"So it is not a matter of any known fact that this killer is a man and not a woman?"

More heads were shaking to answer no.

Rosabelle felt as if she was getting somewhere. "Mrs. Franklin, tell me please, when did Lucy first come into your employ?"

"Early last week . . ." the hostess answered more quietly than usual.

"Do you remember the exact day?"

"Why, let's see . . . let me think . . . what exactly does this all have to do with Mr. Witherspoon?"

"The day, Mrs. Franklin. Please, it could be important."

Mrs. Franklin stared into the distance while counting on her fingers. She tapped her forehead once, which must have worked some miracle, because then she offered an answer. "Tuesday. I think."

"Are you sure?"

"Well . . . yes. Yes, I am sure. I remember. She came to our back door Tuesday morning looking for work after the Pattons had turned her down. I had just come in need as we will be entertaining a house full of visitors from England soon. I learned of the visitors on Monday evening. Yes. It was Tuesday."

Rosabelle was making progress. "So she had been trying to obtain employ in the Patton household? Where Mr. Witherspoon now resides?"

"Yes."

"And does anyone know when the last murder occurred?"

"Oh! I know that one!" The recently married Sarah Pike shot her hand into the air like a schoolgirl bidding anxiously to answer a teacher's question. "My husband knew of this man. They found him dead in his Manassas farmhouse . . . last Monday afternoon!"

Rosabelle grabbed Flora's arm and dragged her down the hall, leaving the group of befuddled women to whisper among themselves. Rosabelle heard Mrs. Franklin mumble something about "that odd girl."

"I am so confused, Rosa," Flora sputtered. "Tell me, please. What is happening?"

"Remember that newspaper story about Abigail Dawes, who was a spy for the South?"

"Yes! We were just speaking to Mr. Witherspoon about her."

"And her favorite disguise was . . ."

"A Negro woman!" Flora stopped just short of the door that opened to the back alley behind the Franklin home. A fresh chill around the area made Rosabelle suspect that someone had just exited through that door.

"Yes. A Negro woman. I think Lucy is Abigail Dawes in disguise."

Flora's eyes grew wide. She pressed a hand to her mouth, stifling a scream.

"Flora, I need you to be strong and do something important for me."

"What?"

"Leave the meeting now. Say you are feeling ill. Run to the police house around the corner and bring them here. I will try to find Lucy and stall her. Make haste!"

"But—"

"Don't argue. Go!"

After Flora scooted off, frazzled but determined, Rosabelle opened the door to the alleyway and poked her head out looking for any sign of Lucy. Nothing. The steps had long been cleared of snow, leaving no chance of tell-tale footprints. She had not given much thought to what action she should take next. Should she search the house, and perhaps find the woman in one of the rooms inside? Or should she look more closely outside? While she stood motionless with indecision, she heard a cracking sound from under the steps. Her heart started beating furiously. Possibly the woman was right below her, hiding.

Rosabelle's respiration grew fast along with her beating heart, and the air filled with her visible breath.

"Miss Raines!" Mrs. Franklin called from the parlor. "Whatever are you doing?"

"Please do not mind me," Rosabelle answered while her fingers turned white from the cold. "I'm stepping outside for a bit of fresh air. I will return in just a moment. Do continue your meeting!"

Rosabelle stepped out onto the landing and closed the door behind her, preempting any argument from Mrs. Franklin about the silly nature of her choice to stand outside in the frigid weather without a cloak. Hoping that it would not be much longer before Flora arrived with the police, Rosabelle decided to venture down the four steep stairs to the muddy ground below. Indeed, once there, she could see faint footprints leading around to the under portion of the staircase. Taking a deep breath and making a silent prayer, she called out.

"I know you are there, Abigail Dawes."

She heard a rustling beneath the stairs.

"Stay away from me if you want to live, Miss Rosabelle Raines. I do not have time for the likes of you," a woman's voice growled.

Fear racing through her veins, Rosabelle took two steps back. She was considering her next course of action when the door above flew open and Flora appeared.

"Rosa! There you are!"

A round and rather squat uniformed policeman squeezed past Flora. At the same time, the small but agile Abigail Dawes sprang out from under the stairs, visibly intent on making a quick getaway. Stopping for just a moment and glaring at Rosabelle, she did not pretend now to avoid eye contact. Her face had been scrubbed clean of whatever she had used to darken it, revealing alabaster skin. Her angry, green eyes bore into Rosabelle's, and Rosabelle shivered not from the cold, but from the chill of hatred that radiated from the woman.

When the policeman started barreling down the stairs, Rosabelle feared Abigail would get away. With no fore-thought, she lunged toward the woman, hoping to grab some part of her dress and hold her back. Abigail Dawes had other plans. Before she knew it, Rosabelle was caught helpless with a knife blade tight against her throat. Abigail Dawes was a master of battle as well as disguise. She had whipped Rosabelle's arm fiercely tight behind her back while positioning the deadly weapon.

The policeman stalled his approach while two more ap-peared in the doorway above. They attempted some verbal negotiations, which had no effect at all on the determined Abigail. The woman began pulling Rosabelle backward, moving ever closer to the busy street at the end of the row of townhouses.

"Stay where you are men, or I will kill her right here, right now."

"It is me that you want, Miss Dawes," said a calm, reso-lute voice behind them. "Leave this woman be."

Rosabelle had only heard that man's voice once, but she knew it to be the voice of Eli Witherspoon.

Abigail whipped around, carrying Rosabelle along for the ride. The forceful movement caused the blade to open her skin, and Rosabelle could feel warm blood trickle down her throat.

"Let her go," Witherspoon pleaded. "I offer myself as a replacement hostage, but please let this woman go." He was so close to them that Rosabelle could see the sweat beading his temple.

Rosabelle knew Abigail was a rat in a trap, and she feared this added to her own danger. She eyed the holstered pistol under Witherspoon's morning coat. Abigail was sharp, so certainly she saw it as well.

"Do you think me a fool, Eli Witherspoon?" Abigail hissed, still twisting Rosabelle to and fro as she looked from Witherspoon to the police and back again.

"I think you are wise enough not to bring harm to this innocent woman."

The twisting stopped. Time seemed to stand still. Rosabelle could barely breathe and felt her world going dark.

Without warning, Abigail loosened her grip on Rosabelle and shoved her into Witherspoon, causing them both to lose balance and fall to the ground. Rosabelle screamed in pain as her arm seemed to snap from the force.

Rosabelle had only a peripheral view of Abigail Dawes fleeing into the street, but during her fall, she heard the loud clatter of hooves on brick, the shrill warning cry of a man, and the screams of onlookers. It was a ghastly sound that Rosabelle imagined she might never forget as long as she lived. On the ground, tangled in the arms of Eli Witherspoon, she was granted relief from witnessing the horses of a carriage trample the avenging woman. Mr. Witherspoon, strong and kind, shielded Rosabelle, making every assurance that once she was able to stand and walk, she would not be forced to view the grisly scene.

Rosabelle would later be told while recovering at home that Abigail did not survive the accident. Over the next few days, Mr. Witherspoon made several visits to the Raines home to check on Rosabelle, whose arm was mending from a severe break acquired during the fall.

Rosabelle worried that Flora would be jealous, but such was not the case. In fact, Flora always smiled and then excused herself from their company in order to allow them the time to be alone.

"Rosa," Flora confided to her sister one day, "Eli Witherspoon is not the man for me. I think he suits you far better."

On quiet walks, he revealed to her his own early suspicions that Abigail Dawes, the Southern Avenger, and the new servant, Lucy, were one and the same. In fact, he told her, he had asked his cousin Amelia not to attend the gathering at the Franklin home for that very reason.

He told her as well, of his life before coming to Alexandria. The stories had been true. Mr. Witherspoon had felt great romantic love for a Negro girl named Bess. They had worked together setting slaves free and transporting them to havens in the North. He believed that all men were God's men, regardless of color, and he would never owe allegiance to a people who would enslave another. When Bess died, he went into hiding until after the war, continuing his work as he was safely able.

It was obvious to everyone that young Mr. Witherspoon had more than just a polite interest in Miss Rosabelle Raines, and that she gladly returned the interest. Before her, she found a compassionate man of staunch integrity, who understood that being different was not a bad thing.

"How did you know?" Eli inquired on one of their walks.

"Know what?" she asked with reserve.

"That Abigail Dawes was hiding disguised in the Franklin home."

"I didn't really know anything. She just . . . acted strangely."

"Strangely?"

"Suspicious . . . I guess. She was acting oddly and . . . I just became curious. That's it. I was curious."

He laughed lightly while sliding Rosabelle a sly glance.

"It seems to me," he teased, "that you know more than you are telling me."

"What in the world could a woman like me know?"

Rosabelle's attempt to act coy was ineffective. "My guess is, Miss Raines, that you are no ordinary woman."

She smiled and guided their conversation toward her companion's new employ in the business of shipping.

One day, Rosabelle knew – one day she could share her own secret with Mr. Eli Witherspoon, and that he would not judge her, think her a witch, or jail her in an asylum.

One day, she could tell him all, and he would embrace her for who she was, and he would love her. That was what Rosabelle knew in her heart.

And time would prove that Rosabelle Raines knew correctly.

"Sherman's Purpose"

BONUS SHORT STORY:

This story is dedicated to my son, Patrick, because it is his favorite

Coffee. Sorry excuse for a beverage, thought Sherman Foster, staring into the empty can. Stuff stank up the house, made his nose itch and his stomach turn.

Resealing the empty container with its plastic lid and shoving it to the back of the counter, Sherman snickered, pleased with himself that he had purposely let the coffee run out. He'd show Horace. Make him real mad, he would. Predictably, Horace would soon yell from his room. "Sherman! Hey, Sherm! Can ya bring me a cup a coffee? My rheumatiz is actin' up."

"Heh, heh," cackled Sherman to himself. "Ain't no coffee ta-day, Horace ol' boy. Guess you'll just have some o' that caffeine withdrawal, 'cuz I ain't goin' out in this weather. Sure enough, I ain't gonna walk half a mile to the Seven Ee-leven, just to get you some stinkin' coffee."

Sherman shuffled slowly on the yellow linoleum floor that, in its heyday, had been the color of soft, speckled cream. For a man his age, a trip from the fridge to the counter was a major undertaking. An arduous ordeal.

Steam blossomed invitingly from the bowl of oatmeal in his hands, stimulating his saliva glands, tempting his taste buds. But halfway to the table, he remembered the honey.

"Damn!" grumbled Sherman to the quiet, friendless kitchen. "Can't eat no bowl of oatmeal without honey."

A mouse on the floor might have heard the scritch-scritching of Sherman's cheap slippers (courtesy the Salvation Army) scuffing the floor as he moved back to the counter where the honey bear bottle colonized with the hen salt shaker and rooster pepper shaker next to the ramshackle gas stove – the same place they'd resided all the years Sherman knew.

Finally, Sherman's bony bottom made contact with the seat of the tippy chair at the small round table. Hunched over the chipped ceramic bowl, holding the bear upside down over the oatmeal, Sherman waited for the honey to drip. He had no choice but to wait. The arthritis made it near impossible to squeeze even the tiniest bit.

Before the honey came, Sherman sighed. He took a peek behind him, down the hallway. "Damn!" he mumbled. "I got oatmeal and I got honey. Horace may be a pain in my ass, but he ain't got no coffee." He shook his head. "Damn, stinkin' coffee."

Flipping the bear back upright, he set it onto the tabletop with a thump. He looked down the hall, sighed one more time, then rose from the chair slow as a sloth and began the long, laborious ritual of bundling up for a cold, even more laborious walk to the Seven Ee-leven.

***

"Hey there, Sherm!" Nancy bellowed from behind the counter. She smiled so broadly that her chubby cheeks pushed her eyes nearly half-closed.

"Damn, Nanc, you look like a crazy China-woman when you smile like that. Anyone ever tell ya that?"

"Why, yes, Sherm," she laughed. "You, as a matter of fact."

"Then why you still do it?"

"To give you sumthin' to complain about." She patted her stomach when she talked and didn't stop smiling. It was Nancy's way.

Evidently, she didn't care if she looked like a crazy China-woman or not.

"So what can we get ya today, Sherm?"

"Can o' Folgers," Sherman answered, shuffling in the same direction as always.

"For Horace?" she asked.

"Who else? I told ya a thousand times, I can't stand the smell of it, much less the taste. Stuff rots your gut." He had made a successful trip to the coffee aisle, picked a can off the shelf and returned to Nancy's register, where he began the slow motion effort of opening his tattered coin purse. "It'll probably kill him," said Sherman, counting out quarters, dimes and nickels one at a time onto the cold counter, "if the laziness don't first. He should be walkin' here himself – get up off his feet ever once in a while. He's just an idiotic old fart. Oughta put him in a home. Let someone else take care of him."

"You love your brother, Sherman Foster. I know ya do." Nancy was getting that sad look on her face again. It bothered Sherman. Sure enough, he didn't like the China-woman look, but that sad-as-a-lost-puppy look was even spookier. Someone really should have a talk with that woman.

He clinked a final coin onto the counter. "That enough, Nanc?"

She counted out the coins, which totaled a dollar fifty-three. The coffee cost three dollars and ninety-nine cents, not including tax.

"That's enough, Sherm," she said. "You be good now. See ya tomorrow?"

"Not if I can help it! This oughta last him least a week for cryin' out loud," moaned Sherman, making his tortoise-like way to the door.

"Right. Well, say 'Hey' to Tina when you see her," said Nancy, who then turned her attention to another customer.

Sherman shook his head and wondered to himself. Tina? Who's Tina?

Snowflakes had started to fall – monstrously luscious snowflakes, floating to the ground like the feathers of angels wings. Once outside, Sherman stopped and looked to the sky. "Snow. Who's gonna shovel this crap? Sure ain't gonna be that lazy bum, Horace."

A young girl stood next to him, looking skyward, eye shining. "I love the snow," she whispered.

Grumbling and angling his head toward the sidewalk he began the long shuffle back to the house where he and his brother had spent years growing from boys to men, so long, long ago.

He passed the big field where they played cops and robbers, and where in winter, they would sail like the wind down the heaven-kissing hill on toboggans. That was when snow was a dream, not a nightmare.

He passed the cemetery where they'd buried Mother, and then Father, who just didn't want to live without her no more.

He passed Pearl O'Leary's house – the woman who broke his heart. Of course, Pearl didn't live there no more, but her granddaughter did, and every once in a while, when she visited the girl, she would stop in and say "Hey!" to Sherman and Horace. She always complimented Sherman on how kind he was to take care of Horace the way he did, bein' like a nurse and all. "You're a good man, Sherman," she'd say.

"Ach – he's a bum. Oughta put him in a home."

"You ain't foolin' me," she'd answer, "You love your brother, Sherman. I know it."

Back in his house, which wasn't much warmer than the air outside, Sherman shook off the snow, hung his ratty coat on its hook, laid his hat and gloves carefully on the radiator nearby, then made his arthritic way to the coffee pot on the stove.

"Hey, Horace!" Sherman shouted down the hall. "You'll have yer stinkin' coffee soon! Don't go yellin' fer it 'cuz I don't wanna hear yer caterwaulin'."

Dog-tired from his grueling walk, Sherman decided to have a sit on the sofa in the living room. Take some weight off his feet for just a few minutes – just while the coffee perked up. As happened on most days, he laid his head down and drifted off.

When Tina came at her usual time, she found a familiar scene – open can of coffee on the counter, a pot percolating furiously over the flame of the single functioning burner left on the stove, and Uncle Sherman asleep on the living room couch.

She took the red can, opened the small door of the pantry, and placed it next to the others that filled the four lined shelves. She counted them. Twenty-one. Twenty-one cans of Folgers. She threw away the empty can, but knew that miraculously, she would find it on the counter when she returned the next day.

After cleaning up, she covered Uncle Sherman with the quilt and waited. When he woke up, she would sit and tell him again. Tell him that Uncle Horace had passed peacefully in his sleep nearly a month ago now. She would ask Uncle Sherman, didn't he remember? Didn't he remember finding Horace in bed that morning, and the lovely funeral when they buried him next to Uncle Fred and Aunt Mimi? Didn't he remember?

Finally, Sherman would shake his head and say that he did. He did remember. He would sit weeping on the couch, his crippled hands cupping his shaking head.

"Why?" he would ask. "Now what'm I gonna do?"

Then he'd curl up in a ball, and sleep again.

Tina would come back. She would come back every day and clean that ancient and tarnished coffee pot. After all, it was his purpose – making coffee for the brother he loved.

Everyone who knew Sherman knew the truth. That those two had been more than brothers – they'd been best friends. And they knew that despite his cranky grumbling, Sherman Foster really had loved Horace all the years that he lived.

Loved him more than a child loves the sight of new falling snow.

Were you entertained?

I hope so! For more Barbara Marr fun, consider reading

Take the Monkeys and Run and *Citizen Insane*

Made in the USA
Charleston, SC
04 May 2014